Taken by a Vampire

Remy Marie

Published by Remy Marie, 2023.

This is a work of fiction. Similarities to real people, places, or events are entirely coincidental.

TAKEN BY A VAMPIRE

First edition. October 5, 2023.

Copyright © 2023 Remy Marie.

ISBN: 979-8223271789

Written by Remy Marie.

Table of Contents

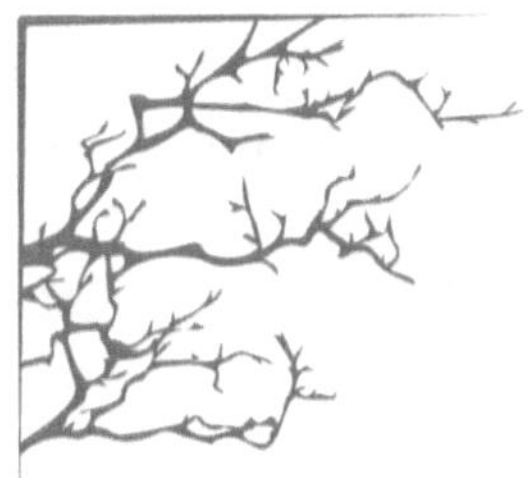

Chapter 1

Zane

I love the night. I love the sounds, the cool air on my cheek, and the neon glow lighting everything up. There is nothing like it. From my perch, one thousand feet up, I feel like a God. For the last three hundred years, I've watched this city grow into the grand landscape of what it is today.

New York City, there's nothing like it.

Every night, I choose the highest building, sit, and listen to the city. Normal human ears wouldn't be able to pick up the sounds I hear from this distance, but for a vampire, I can hear it all. The cars honking, the New Yorkers arguing, the rats shuffling, and even the roaring subway, thirty feet below ground level. Each sound is like an instrument in a beautiful orchestra. I love this city.

Stretching, I leap from my current post and shift to a building fifty feet away. Landing with a *whump*, I crotch back down, and continue to search for my next meal.

I am so damn hungry. It's been days since I've had my last decent meal. This city isn't what it used to be. Decades ago, this city at night was like an all you can eat buffet, full of criminals and rapists, but now this city is a nurtured beast, filled with business moguls and generation Z TikTokers. *Ugh.*

I shift my position again. This time I run across the building's railing, then leap to a lower building below it. I land with ease as I continue my search for food.

Running, I hear a female scream, "Help! Get off me! Somebody help me!"

A smile parts my face, "Dinner is served."

Without a care for the height that I am at, I jump from the building and transform into my bat. Like an eagle, I fly with haste to the sound of the woman's plea. When I arrive to the alley, I spot a blonde woman, pin to a wall by a large man. Behind him, are two others laughing. Wanting to get a better understanding of the situation, I hover above, surveying my next meal.

It's clear the large man, pinning the woman down is the leader. With his slicked back auburn hair, leather jacket, worn jeans and boots, I would guess he was a motorcycle gang member and behind him must be his crew, bad guy number one and two.

A three course meal, perfect.

My eyes switch to the blonde on the wall, and I nearly fall in mid flight. She is gorgeous. Bright blonde hair, golden skin, and a natural curvy body. Looking at her in her tight teal mini dress, I forget the reason for me being there.

"Aww, come on baby. The more you move. The more this is going to hurt. Just let me and my friends have a go at you, then it would all be over."

Struggling, the blonde woman, punches the large one, causing him to stumble backwards.

"Perhaps she doesn't need saving after all. There's fight in her." I admire from above.

Freed, she runs away from the gang, but she didn't get far as the others grab her arms.

"You bitch!" He shouts, blood dripping through his fingers.

The smell alone causes my stomach to growl.

"That's going to leave a mark, you stupid cunt! I was going to let you off easy. But now. Now, I'm going to make you pay. Boys, hold her."

The young woman attempts to break their hold, but the two out match her, freezing her in place.

"Oh, baby, I'm going to make you pay." Hiking her skirt above her waist, he traces his finger across her soft porcelain skin, slipping it under her lace panties. She screams from his touch, but in response, he laughs.

"Shhh...Scream all you want. There isn't a soul that can save you," he says, unbuckling his belt.

I shift back into my human form and land behind him.

"Now gentleman, that's no way to treat a beautiful lady."

The gang member turns, his eyes grow wide and his jaw drops.

"Where did that black guy come from?"

"It doesn't really matter, where I came from. What matters is you're *mine.*"

With a swift punch, my fist goes straight through the gang members chest and I pull out his beating heart. I could feel the blood leak from the organ, as the leader stared at me like a ghost.

"Wha-" His last words are futile, as his lifeless body falls like a sack. I lick the heart, drinking the warm blood it contains, and my body tingles from the wonderful copper taste.

Looking at their fallen comrade, the two goons stare at each other and then at me.

"What the fuck! You killed Aaron! I'll kill you, motherfucker!"

Clearly not paying attention to my enhanced abilities the fools attempt to fight me in hand to hand combat. I dodge the attacks, batting away their fists with ease. Looking over to the woman, I notice she's still clinging to the wall. Her eyes never leaving Aaron's corpse.

"Hey!" I shout.

Her blue eyes leave the dead body to look at me. Upon eye contact, I froze. I've never seen such bold blue eyes before. They are like the ocean, so vast and deep.

Caught in her beauty, a goon manages to lay a punch on me. My body didn't move from the impact, but the goon screams bloody murder, clutching his fist and falling to to his knees.

"Yeah, that's broken. My bones, they may feel like steel to your hands. Sorry about that." Grabbing him by the collar, I shove him into a wall. From the impact, I hear his bones crack.

Two down one to go.

The last one attempts to punch me, but I dodge his attack again, and push him to the side. He collides hard into the ground, and doesn't get back up. I know he's still alive because I can hear his heartbeat. I'll save him for later, but for now it's time to play the hero.

"Are you alright? You're safe now." I want to tell her to leave and run to safety, but yet I feel called to her. I'm called to her in a way that I've never been before.

Is it possible that her beauty alone can reignite a dead heart?

No, you can't. Remember there are laws. The humans can never know our true existence, even though this one manages to make me flutter.

"I'm alright." Her eyes never left the leader's open chest wound.

"Hey," I repeat. I touch her chin and move her blue eyes towards mine. Her eye line adjusts and focuses on me. "What's your name?"

"Hannah."

"Hannah, my name is Zane. I'm an uncover cop with NYPD. Right now you are going through a traumatic experience. Things are not as they seem."

"You're a cop..." she mutters. Her eyes glance away from mine, back to the crippled bodies behind me.

"Hannah, look at me!" I touch her chin once more, bringing her vision back in line with mine.

Mind compulsion only works as long as her eyes are locked with my own.

"Yes, I'm a cop. I had to shoot those men before they hurt you. What is important now is that your safe. You must leave and never tell anyone about what happened tonight, as you will comprise our undercover operation. Repeat after me."

If she repeats my words, she will be compelled to lie and her memory of this night will be gone. I have her where I want her.

"I will not-"

"Fuck you! You motherfucker!"

My senses scream as hear a gun click. Turning around, I see the last gang member with a pistol in his hand. At the sound of the trigger being pulled, I lean my body, dodging the shot. In milliseconds, I close the gap between us and squeeze his throat.

It was stupid not to kill him earlier.

With pop, I break his spine, and he falls lifeless to the ground.

Staring at him, I hear a small peep behind me, "Officer..."

I turn to see Hannah clutching her stomach, with blood leaking through her fingers.

"Shit, no, no!" I catch her before she falls. Cradling her in my arms, with her head resting on my thighs, I push her blonde hair behind her ear. The blue eyes that were once full of life fades quickly.

"I don't want to die. I don't want to die. I'm so scared." She cries. Tears roll down her cheeks, as she grabs my shirt sleeve. Looking down at her, I feel helpless. I didn't want her to die either. It was my fault she got shot. If I hadn't played with my food, she would still be alive. Damnit. Why was I so reckless?

"Please help..." She croaks. Blood now leaked out of her mouth, which meant her lungs are full of blood. There is only a short amount of time before she dies. I have to do something. Her arms grasp my shirt frantically, as she drowns in her own blood. She begins to cough, and her eyes scream out a final desperate plea.

Looking at her blue eyes, I growl, "Fuck the bylaws."

My canines grow to become fangs and I bite into her neck.

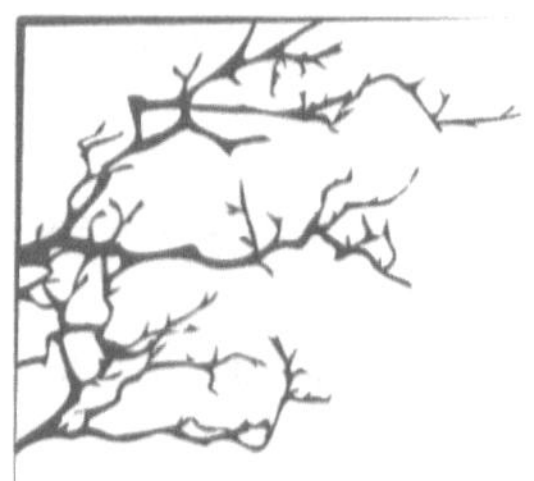

Chapter 2

Hannah

The sound of two voices jolted my eyes open. Both have heavy African dialects as they spoke quickly. I groan and palm by forehead, trying to soothe the pain from the splitting headache that is beating my brain like a drum. Every inch of my body is in pain, even the small hairs in my body are aching.

How many drinks did I have last night? This is the last time, I drink away my guy problems.

I shift in the bed I am in, and sit up. My heart drops, as I realize I'm still wearing my mini dress from the night prior and didn't recognize my surroundings.

Where the hell am I? Please don't tell me I slept with someone.

I attempt to get my barring of the room, but it's so dark, that I could barely see my hand in front of me. With my hand still up, the room slowly became more visible as if someone is using a light dimmer. Soon, not only is my hand visible, the entire room is lit up as if there is a light turned on, but there isn't a light present in the dark cavernous room.

"What?" I breathe. Seconds ago, it's too dark to see an inch of front of me, but now I can see my hand in front of me, hell I can see the entire room.

Looking around, I see that it's a windowless room with stone grey walls, with a bookcase, and a table with two antique chairs near the left wall. I am in the center of the room in a wooden sleigh bed with red silk sheets.

"Where the hell am I?" I question. A loud growl, draws my attention to the door in front of me.

"What in the hell were you thinking?"

"She was going to die, I had to save her!"

"At the cost of what, Zane? Did you tell her? Did you tell her what she was fated to for eternity?"

"No, but Oye, you don't understand. She was going to die. I had to-"

Who was going to die? Was he referring to me? A fuzzy memory of a dream fades through my mind. I was being pinned to a wall, and three men tried to rape me. I was then saved by this man. He was super fast and strong like a superhero. Then there was a gun shot and I was bleeding.

I look down at my teal dress and saw the crimson stain. My body began to tremble, as I inspect the ripped cloth. It's small enough to stick my index finger through. A perfect size for a bullet.

The gunshot...was that not a dream?

"Save your words, brother. We have lived for centuries, and have seen many die. Why is this the first human you suddenly feel pity for? Father, will not tolerate this. You know he would have liked to be consulted before...UGH! Do you even know what you've done? Do you understand that as a vampire, we are only allowed to change one human in our lifetime, and that person that we change is our mate forever? What do you know of her, hmm?"

"Her name is Hannah..."

My mouth drops.

He is referring to me. Wait, does that mean that I'm a vampire? Vampires don't exist. They only exist in movies and steamy romance novels. This is just a dream. Well, a dream within a dream. Those exist right? Inception showed that this is possible. You just need to wake up. You're going to wake up. Hopefully...

"Just a name, baby brother? Just a name? That is all you know about her? How foolish are you?"

"She was shot! She was going to die in that alleyway!"

I look back down at my blood stained dress. The hole the bullet left was still visible, however my skin was completely healed. There's not even a scar. How is that possible?

"So you let her die! Humans are for substance, nothing else. Brother, there are rules of engagement for finding a human mate. She hasn't passed any of the trials, met our family, nor received approval to be turned. You disobeyed our laws. You do know what this means, brother? The punishment for turning a human without permission."

"Death by combat versus the tribe's champion."

"Yes, and who is tribe's champion?"

"You."

"Exactly! So even if I go along with this charade, in the end, one of us will be dead, and I certainly don't plan on dying so early in life, brother. Damnit. I am so frustrated right now, I can't even look at you. Have you..." Oye paused her speech. "She's awake."

I quickly attempt to act like I've just woken, but let's face it, I'm sure they knew I was listening to their conversation. The door opens and Zane and Oye walk in. They are obviously siblings as their ebony skin and facial features of a large nose and high cheekbones match. Both have athletic bodies, but Zane is a head taller than his sister. Based on what they are wearing, I'm not sure if it's the night or morning as Zane is shirtless with a black robe and a pair of silk slacks, and his sister is wearing a ruby evening gown.

"Good Morning Hannah," Zane says, approaching the bed. "I'm sure you have a lot of questions."

I'm not sure why, but instinctively I pull the covers over my body and inch backwards towards the bed's headboard. Zane stops his encroachment and bit his lip. Beside him, Oye shakes her head, sighs, and crosses her arms.

"I'm not going to hurt you," he says slowly. I eyeball his sister and he reads my timidness. "My sister isn't going to harm you neither." He looks towards his sister and she sighs once more and walks out of the room.

"It's just you and me now." He replies once the door is closed. He places his palms up, signaling his innocence.

I still don't feel right with him. He has a friendly smile, but I know nothing about him. His meaty, hulk-like exterior is threatening, yet his soft brown eyes are like an innocent puppy. I am caught in a whirlwind of confusion and curiosity, I'm eager to learn the next chapter, yet scared to move on. I stay silent as our eyes remain locked.

"Well, I'm sure this is a lot to take in so, I'll just speak. If at anytime you have a question, interrupt me. Do you understand?"

I don't move. I sit frozen in place. This bed might be foreign and new to me, but suddenly I feel like it is safer than my own home.

"Right...so...last night, you were attacked."

So it's true about the memories of those men. Everything is true.

"I managed to save you, but I was foolish and let my guard down. One of your attackers pulled a gun and shot towards me. I dodged the bullet, but you were behind me and got caught in the cross fire." He pauses and sighs. "Hannah, if I would have known that you were behind me, I would have never moved. I would have took the bullet, but once again, I was a fool. You were dying and I had to make a choice. I chose to turn you."

"Turn me to what?" I ask. I know the answer, but I have to hear it again.

"A vampire," he says. On cue, his brown eyes disappeared and became pitch black and long fangs appeared in his mouth. I shriek at the eerie sight. I've never seen something more devilish looking before. Sensing my discomfort, Zane transforms back to his human form.

"Are you saying I can do that?"

"Yes, like me, you are gifted with untold strength, speed and stamina. With practice, you will be able to transform into a bat as well."

I snort at the last part. "A bat? Really?"

"Yes, what is so funny about that?"

"Nothing, I guess. It's just that you have a body of a guy who lives in a gym, and just imagining you turn into teeny tiny bat is humorous."

He bit his lip, but soon a smile spread on his face, and he began to laugh too.

"I guess that is funny in its own way." He rubbed the back of his shaved head, then pointed to the corner of the bed that is opposite of me. "May I sit?"

I nod, feeling more comfortable with him.

Sitting down, his eyes are more heavier than before, as if his next words are dire. "Hannah this next part will come to a shock to you and I accept any reactions that come from it. All I ask is you be honest with me. Deal?"

I nod.

"In our race, to turn someone, we separate part of our soul, and transfuse it into a human. Once we bite a human, we are mates for life. If we attempt to create another mate, we will die from the transfusion. Which is why turning a human into a vampire is such a big deal. When I created that bond between us, I can never take it back. We are connected forever."

"When you say mate, you mean like were married?"

"In a way, yes. As my mate, we are required to repopulate our race with offspring."

I gulp and shift my position in the bed, bringing my knees to my chest. I look down at the red silk sheets and pushed my blonde curls behind my ear.

"And let me guess, sex is the only way to do this."

"Yes. We breed like normal humans."

"So I'm like a sex slave to you or something?"

"No, not at all. You are free to do whatever you choose."

"So I can go?"

"No, I'm afraid it's not that easy. You are a vampling or freshly turned. You are not able control your hunger yet. Leaving could be dangerous for you and your loved ones."

"I can't see any of my friends and family any more?"

"I'm afraid not. It's too dangerous, you run the risk of killing them by accident. Oye and I are your family now."

My mouth feels dry. Drier than usual as if a rock is stuck in my throat. How can I start a brand new life and not be able to see my family or my friends, like Ash and Terry? I didn't even get a chance to say goodbye. How can I adopt this new lifestyle if I wasn't the one who even chose it for me? Even more, I am wishing this is all a dream. A horrible, horrible dream that I will wake up from.

"I feel your pain and I understand it. All of this is a big change," Zane said. He scoots closer to me, and grabs my hand. His skin feels so cold and dry. It's unnatural. His brown eyes pierce into my own as he massages my small ivory hand in his large russet one.

"You do not know how I feel," I snap. I attempt to break my hand out of his grasp, but he's too strong as he continues to hold my hand.

"I sense you are going through an array of emotions. You are angry, confused, and sad, but mostly you are afraid. You are not afraid of me, or this new form you have taken. No, you are afraid of something more simpler. You are upset that you did not have a chance to say goodbye to your loved ones."

"How did you..."

"We are more connected than just a normal human marriage bond. When we transfused, you transferred your essence into me, as I did.

With that I am able to sense your emotions, I can tell when you are afraid, angry , or happy. As you can for me."

"What if I don't want to me mated to you. I'm only twenty-two. I have my whole life ahead of me."

"That is your choice. However, that is a lonely choice. Attempting to have a relationship with a human, only drives our hunger, and you run the risk of killing that loved one. And any attempt to mate with another vampire, you will be shunned. As in the eyes of many you are already claimed."

"Claimed? Like I'm your damn property?"

My cheeks are burning with rage as I stare at him. My hands ball into a fists, and my mouth sags to a frown. I don't think Zane needs our emotional connection to tell that I'm pissed. I have to get out of here. I need to run away. There's no way in hell, I will ever be with this man.

"Hannah-" he reaches up to touch my shoulder, but I pull away.

"Don't touch me. Don't you dare think for a second that what you did is okay. Thank you for saving me, but forcing me to take this life. I cannot do this. I have friends and family back home. They are probably worried sick about me. I'm sorry, but I have to go. I can't be here." I hop out of the bed and he chases after me.

"Hannah, please stop."

"Stay away from me Zane!" Running barefoot, I navigate my way through several rooms. I have no idea if I'm going the right direction as every room I pass through didn't have a window. Eventually, I ran to a heavy wooden door. The door is larger than others and looks more decorative than the others too. Grabbing the large iron ring, I pull it open and a blinding bright light engulfs the dark room. I growl as the white light stuns my vision.

In the background I can hear, Zane shout, "Hannah stop. You mustn't go outside."

I have to leave. I have to escape. I didn't want this. I didn't want any of this.

Not heeding his warning, I step outside, into the daylight. I only take one step in the sunlight and I fall to my knees screaming bloody murder. It hurt so much. My lungs burn while my skin feels like it's lit on fire. White hot searing pain covers my entire body, and I'm immobile, praying that the pain will end. Looking up, I see Zane's face. He's in equal pain as he hovers over me. His face is boiling, his skin is raw, pink and burned as if someone pour hot acid over it.

"I gotcha." He growls in pain. Gritting his teeth together, he lifts me up, and drags me back inside and shuts the door.

With his back on the door, he grins, "Don't do that again..." his words are his last as he slips into unconscious.

"Zane!" I shout, before I too slip into blackness.

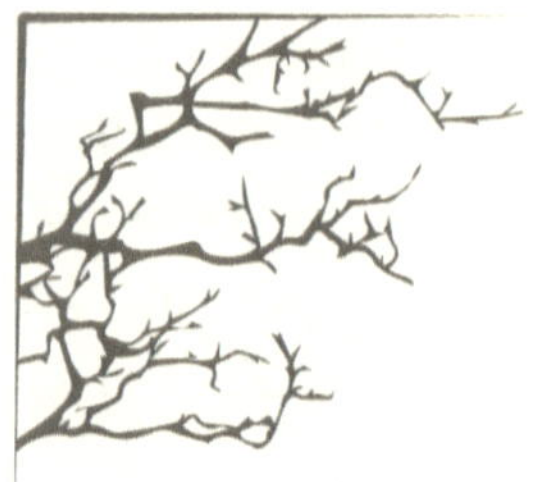

Chapter 3

Zane

"How is she?" I ask, staring at the unconscious body of my mate. Her skin is raw and pink with pieces of black charred scabs are covering in her skin in various places.

"She's a fighter. A stupid fighter, but a fighter. How are you healing?"

"I'm in better shape than her. I took less sunlight than she did. My back still hurts and I'm afraid I may have to use this cane to get around till I'm fully healed."

"It was an admirable thing you did. Foolish, but admirable." Oye laughs to herself and shakes her head. "Look at you, you're already showing signs of devotion. Perhaps we can trick father into thinking that this was a sudden romance."

"She's the blood of my blood. That is all. There will be nothing romantic growing between us." I stare at her body, while she is beautiful, it would be unfair to force a relationship on her. I would rather spend an eternity alone than to force another to love me. That's not love, that's slavery.

"Brother, did you hear me?"

"What?"

"I asked if you could bring me another bag of blood. She's healing slower than I thought."

"Yes, of course." I groan as I use the cane to hobble to the blood refrigerator in the healing room.

Like the rest of the Adebayo Manor, it's quiet, dark, and old. Filled with various antique furnishings and tribal decorations from my ancestors.

Grabbing a bag of A positive, my favorite blood type, I toss it across the room to my sister, and she catches it with one hand. Ripping it open with her fangs, she squeezes the liquid into my mate's mouth.

"Remind me brother, why did she run out in the daylight? You did tell her that we are vulnerable to sunlight, right?"

"I didn't get a chance too. She ran out before I could say something."

My sister looks at me. Her scowl tells me her current temperament.

"She's frighten. The fact that she's a vampire is a shock to her," I plea.

"I heard the conversation brother. It wasn't about the fact that she's a vampire. It's the fact that she found out that she's bounded to you for life. That is what shocked her. This is why, we have rules for mating! Father raised you better."

"Mother also raised me to care for others too. Especially humans."

Oye goes silent at the mention of our mother. We don't talk about her like we should. She brushes off the memory and narrows her eyes.

"Humans are cattle to us. Nothing more. Never confused that fact, brother. Sometimes I can't believe we are blood. It looks like that second bag of blood is doing it's trick, her skin is starting to heal. She will need more to be at full strength. It looks like you could use some more blood too."

"I'm fine," I growl.

"Fine, but you can't deny that you need blood. It's nearly night, brother. Perhaps it's time to take her out on her first hunt. Warm fresh blood heals better than this bagged cold horseshit.

I shake my head, "she's not ready."

"She needs to be. She needs to learn how to properly hunt and kill. She's your problem. Deal with it." Oye walked towards her cloak and tossed it over her shoulders. After looking in the mirror, she looked back at me. "I'm leaving to meet father at the Elders conference. I'll keep your little secret to myself when I meet him, but he will want to see you when we return. It's been two decades since he's seen either of us. When he arrives at the manor is when he will meet her." Oye nods towards Hannah. My sister growls and pushes back her natural ebony curls.

"Get her in line. Teach her our ways. Perhaps we can pass her off. Father and I will return within three months, you have till then to train her. Take care brother." Oye said, putting the hood of her cloak up.

"You as well sister." Oye nodded then left me alone with Hannah.

Hannah screams, jolting awake.

"It's okay, just calm down," I comfort her. Looking at me, she shrieks and scrambles to the corner of the bed.

"I'm not going to hurt you."

"Stay away from me!"

"Hannah, please. You must calm down."

"Just leave me."

"Hannah, you are weak and injured. The only way you can heal is to listen to me."

"Why should I listen to you? I don't even know you."

"Argh!" I growl. I rub my shaved head and walk away. I can't look at her at the moment. I point a finger at her and yell, "Damnit woman! If you are going to be stubborn and deny my help, then STARVE!" My voice is full of rage. I know I must be a scary site as I feel my outstretch fangs resting on my lips. I don't care. Though I may look like a devil spawn from hell, I know I am no monster. A monster would have left her alone to bleed out in that alleyway.

Lowering my voice, I attempt to sound less hostile. It's hard, because her fearful face only fuels my discontent.

"I am not here to have my way with you nor rape you or eat you. I am trying to help you. I've saved your life twice in the last twenty four hours and the only gratitude I've received is rejection. For the last time, I have no interest in being romantic with you. However, for the sake of both our lives, you must cooperate and listen to me. At this point, I rather face my sister in the combat pit, than deal with your annoying timidness. When you are ready to be civilized come and find me. Till then, you are on your own. It is the night now, and I'm not stopping you from leaving the manor. The door is right there, you are free to leave. What is your choice? Are you staying or going?"

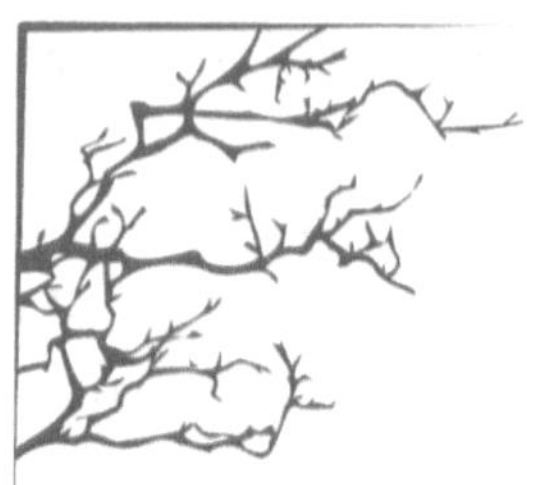

Chapter 4

Hannah

I didn't have to look at him to feel his raw emotions. Anger. Regret. Fear. Loneliness. Each one feels like a powerful punch to my gut. His emotions are suffocating me to the point where I'm hyperventilating like I have asthma. I place a hand on my chest, trying to get my emotions under control.

I can't explain it but I start to cry from the pressure of my choice. Normally, I wouldn't be crying. Especially over a guy, but right now, I've never felt more depressed. The gravity of the situation feels like a anchor sinking me down at sea. I am drowning in emotion, unable to deal with the choice at hand. I don't know this man at all, but yet there is a calling for me to stay with him. Is it strange to say that in my heart, I want to be with him?

Wiping my tears away, I question why am crying. I feel so connected to him, yet I don't know a thing about him. It's a weird unexplainable connection, feeling as if I just broke up with my best friend and watched my dog die in the same day. Thinking of friends, I realize that my best friend, Ash, would be worried sick since I haven't checked in since the club last night.

"I want to leave." I answer. I can see the disappointment wash over his face. It's not hard to spot. Even if we didn't share emotions, I could tell that he is unhappy with my answer.

"I'm sorry, I have to check in with my friends. I just can't disappear without telling them first."

Zane nods and then sighs , "Well if you're going to leave you're going to need a change of clothes. If someone sees you in a bloody dress, you'll get more questions than you want."

"Thank you." I reply, feeling relief that he will not hold me captive.

"I'll be right back. Hold on." He left the room and in ten minutes he returned with several items in his hands. He was carrying a pair of jeans, a green sweater, white sneakers and a black book bag.

"Here are some of my sisters clothes. I'm sure she won't mind. I also brought you a bag to put your dirty clothes in. Inside the bag is a cell phone with my number programmed in too. If you need anything, call me."

I nod taking the clothes from him. Hopping off the table, I grab the strap of my dress but notice his eyes were still on me. Our eyes fall into a deep stare, neither of us wavering. Zane coughs and looks away.

"Sorry for staring. Your beauty is one of a kind. I'll leave the room so that you can have your privacy."

I didn't know what to say. I could tell that he truly meant what he said. The way he looks at me makes me feel like I'm the only woman in the world.

"Thank you."

Zane nods and then leaves the room. Once he is gone, I quickly shed the dress off and place on the jeans and sweater. The jeans are a bit tight, but they fit. Picking the dress off the ground, I stare once again at the bullet hole. I still can't believe that I was shot. It's an amazing feat that I'm alive right now. Even though, I'm this horrible monster, if Zane didn't interfere I would had been dead. Mate for life or not, I owe him a huge amount of gratitude.

Hearing a knock, I look away from my dress and say, "I'm dressed. You may enter."

Zane peeks his head in and smiles. "Perfect fit."

"Thanks," I say, looking down, adjusting the sleeves.

The way he looks at me makes my insides quiver every time. He may say that there's nothing between us, but his stares tell a different story.

Zane takes the book bag and opens it indicating that I should throw in my dress. I toss it in and he then walks to a large refrigerator in the room. He takes out two red bags and tosses it into the book bag. After zipping it up, he grabs another plastic bag from the fridge and walks back.

"Here," he says handing it to me. Upon closer inspection, I realize what the mysterious crimson liquid is.

"Blood?" I ask.

"It's the only way we can stay strong."

"As vampires, we're undead, so normal human means of substance don't matter to us like hunger and thirst, this gives us unnatural eternal life. The only thing that can kill us is sunlight or a beheading."

"Not a wooden stake to the heart?"

"Made up fairy tales. We are already dead. Why would a stab wound kill us? A dumb rumor started by humans."

"So we're pretty much immortal?"

Zane nods and then says, "We can go years without a drop of blood, but a vampire who hasn't eaten is weaken. And if we're weak, we can't defend ourselves."

"Defend ourselves against who?"

"As vampires our greatest enemy is also our one food source, humans. You mustn't allow them to learn of our existence. By doing so you threaten our entire race. Humans are naturally destructive and if they learn about us they will hunt us to the last vamp. Nothing is more dangerous than when humans are united against one threat."

"What about my friends? I trust them. They won't-"

"Hannah, please. It's different now. Trust me. You are free to leave, but please don't go back to your old life. Stick to low populated areas for now until you can control your hunger. You are still a vampling.

Being around that many humans will be too much temptation. You can kill someone if you're not too careful and that only draws more attention."

I open my mouth to dispute him, but he shakes his head, clearly reading my mind on my thoughts. Sighing, I cross my arms and stare at the blood he gave me.

"Fine." I lie. "So, what am I supposed to do with this?"

"I want you to drink it. You're too weak right now to leave, but after this last bag, you should be ready to go."

I nod and stare at the bag. It's squishy and cool. My eyes trails the air pocket inside the amber colored bag.

"How do I...how do I drink blood?"

"Open the bag and the smell of it will do the rest." He replies.

I nod and rip the plastic. Zane is right, as the moment the metallic scent hits my nose I could feel a change in my body. My teeth start to grow and my body feels more alive than previously. The longer I stare at the open container, the greater my hunger grows.

It's an unbearable, feeling as if I haven't eaten in a day. Unable to wait any longer, I shove the bag in my mouth. The crimson liquid tastes like sweet lemonade on a hot summer day as I drink it. Feeling more hungrier than usual, I shove the bag in my mouth trying to drink the entire contents in one sip.

"Drink it slowly." Zane instructs me.

Reaching out he attempts to grab the blood from me, but instinctively I take a step back. I look at him and admit a low growl. He doesn't seem threatened by my sudden aggressive manner. I finish the bag, but I still feel hungry.

"Here," Zane says handing me another bag. "Remember drink slowly. If you drink too fast you will become blood crazed. Blood crazed vampires are dangerous as nothing can stop them. All they want is blood. We only need three pints of blood a day. For healing we need twice that amount. A blood crazed vampire is different though. You are animalistic and you can't stop your actions. All you want is blood, and you will kill hundreds of humans to fill your lust. The only way to stop a blood crazed vamp is death."

I nod and calm myself down before drinking the next bag. I drink it more slowly this time and I strangely feel full afterwards.

Zane nods and smiles, "Good. If you run out of blood, call me and I'll bring you more. Or go to the hospital and tell them you are with the Adebayo tribe. They should know what to do next."

"You mean, I don't need to kill anyone?"

"I prefer if you don't. Since you chose to leave, I don't have time to properly train you to hunt and kill for substance. It's too risky. For now, only fight for defense. Any more questions?"

I shake my head and look down at my newly acquired shoes. They feel foreign to me. Hell, all of this feels foreign to me. I feel like I'm still in a dream, and the body that I'm in doesn't belong to me. None of this makes any sense. Two days ago, I was dealing with a break up and now, I'm a vampire. Life has its fucked up moments, and this is definitely one of them.

I feel nervous about going out on my own. As I grind my feet in the ground, I feel Zane's hands on my shoulders. His touch is powerful yet gentle, and from it, I feel relief.

"Hannah," He says softly lifting my chin up to meet his vision.

Listening to him say my name in his husky African accent gives me goosebumps.

"I'm not going to argue about your decision, but know that I'm here for you. You have my number. If you need me. Call me. Okay?"

I nod. After taking a deep breath, I look into his brown eyes and say, "Thank you. For everything."

"You're welcome. Now go. You're wasting the night."

I nod and head to the door. As I grab the door handle, I feel a sudden rush of sadness. I know it isn't my emotions, it's his.

I want to look back, but I know if I did, I'll be tempted to stay.

Walking out of the room, I head back to the large doors that I attempted to escape from earlier. Opening the door, this time is different than the last. Instead of searing hot pain, cool wind brushes past my cheek as I stare at the dark starry night. Looking at only trees, I realize that I'm no longer in the city.

Leaving the mansion, I walk through the property's gardens, to a large iron gate, finding myself at what looks like the main road.

"Alright, so first things first. I need a ride." I open my bag and take out my phone preparing to call my friend Ash to pick me up. As I stare at the flip phone, I curse underneath my breath realizing that I don't know my friends number by heart.

Curse my smartphones contacts numbers!

"And I guess an Uber is out of the question too, since this ancient flip phone can't download apps. Figures. Zane would give a phone not from this decade. I didn't even know they still made flip phones." I mutter.

I open the phone's contacts to only see Zane's number. The longer I stare at the number the more I question if I should even leave.

Zane is right. My prior life is over. I can't expect my life to continue like it did before. How do I explain to my love ones that I can only eat blood? Not the mention the whole I can't walk in sunlight without barbecuing thing. None of it is practical. Should I go back?

I turn and face the the four story sandstone mansion weighting my options.

What about Ash though? She's been my friend since fourth grade. She needs to know that I'm alive. Perhaps, I can stop by her place first, say my goodbyes then leave. Then what about my parents, do I need to call them too?

No, since our falling out five years ago neither of us have spoken to each other. Perhaps it's better just to let them live their lives like before.

So then what's the plan? Speak to Ash then come back here? I'm sure Zane would be happy on my return. Perhaps, by returning, I can get these newly acquired powers under control. Then I can visit Ash daily.

I smile at the thought as I walk out the gate, and head down the street.

After thirty minutes of walking in the dark, I hear a car engine in the distance. Looking behind me, I expect to see a car pass me, but there isn't a vehicle near me. The noise grows louder with every second and I began to hear other noises too. For instance, I could hear two people speak, breathe, hell I can even hear their blood pumping through their body.

That is the freaky part, as I am drawn to the sound of their blood pumping. Listening, I stand frozen on the side of the road. The longer I listen, I feel my stomach growl and shake. Even after drinking the two bags of togo blood, I'm still hungry. When a pair of headlights blind me, I wake up from my zombie hunger state.

Sticking my thumb out, I hope the driver will stop for me. After driving past me, the car stutters to a stop and pulls over to the side of the road. A smile breaks on my face as I run up to the stopped truck.

"Oh, thank you!" I say in relief.

"Are you alright, ma'am?" An older gentleman asks. Sitting beside him is an older lady with an equal look of worry on her face.

"I am. I just need a ride. Where am I?"

"You're in Northridge. About fifty miles away from New York City." He replies.

"Is everything alright? Do we need to get the sheriff?" She asks.

"No, I just need a ride. Could you take me to Midtown in the city."

The couple looked at each other then discuss among themselves. The older lady then smiles at me and said, "You're in luck. We're heading to the Upper West Side to visit our daughter, we'll give you a ride. Hop in."

Grinning, I walk to the rear door of the four door vehicle and get inside.

"Thank you," I reply, buckling myself in. The older gentleman starts the car and drives towards the highway.

"Name's John and this is my wife Elizabeth."

"Hello," Elizabeth chimes, sticking her hand out to shake.

"Hello, I'm Hannah." I reply, shaking her hand.

After smiling at me, Elizabeth says, "Are you hungry dear? We have an extra burger."

"No, I'm fine." Usually the thought of a juicy fast food burger would make my mouth water, but I now found my tastes wanting something different. The thought of food reminded me how hungry I've become since I've joined the older couple.

"Hannah, what brings you outside at this time a night? A young lady like yourself shouldn't be walking alone like that. It's dangerous. Is everything alright?"

"Yeah, everything is fine. Just boy troubles. I had to get out of there if you know what I mean."

"Oh, I do, but at this time of night you shouldn't be walking alone. You should have called for a taxi. There's murders and rapists about. You should be thankful that we found you and not some manic."

"Aww shucks, Elizabeth you know there's no criminals in this town. It's quieter than a church mouse here. You're only thinking of the city."

"No, just last week there was a robbery down on Main at Bob's shop."

"Right a robbery. Not a murder. You make it sound like Northridge is the southside of Chicago."

"All I'm saying is that..."

I smile at the older couple bickering. The longer the two argue about the safety of their small town, the more I notice their blood pump quicker. It is slow at first, however the longer the two argue, the faster their blood flows. I try to ignore it, but the beat continues to get harder and harder to ignore. Looking forward, my enhanced vision notices Elizabeth's artery in her neck. From my seat, I could see it vibrate as she talks to her husband. My stomach growls the longer I stare at her neck.

I'm so damn hungry. The longer I stare the more hungrier I get. I open my bag to grab a bag of blood but I'm disappointed when I notice there is nothing but empty containers.

"Shit." I whisper, digging through he bag, hoping to find another full bag of blood.

"Is everything alright back there?"

"Yeah. Just trying to find something." I reply, shifting the contents around. When my hand comes up empty, I curse underneath my breath again. The hunger is unbearable and the sound of Elizabeth's blood beating didn't help.

I attempt to think of other things, like walks on the beach, music, or good sex. None of it works. The only thing that was on my mind was sinking my teeth into Elizabeth's neck. I have to have her. I can't take it any more.

In a spilt second, I unbuckle my seat belt and attack her. Both of them are surprised by my actions. Elizabeth screams as my teeth dig into her skin. Her warm blood tastes so good as I drink from her. My brain is shouting this is wrong and that I'm killing her, yet my animalistic side of me is craving substance. I can't control myself.

"What in God's name! Get off her you fucking psycho!"

John attempts to attack me, but his punches feel like soft air touching my skin. Not leaving her neck, I push John hard into the window. I hear the window crack and John utter in pain.

From my actions, John releases the steering wheel causing the vehicle to skid off the road and flip off the highway. As the car doubles over, I never let go of Elizabeth's neck. With both hands, I shove her neck deeper into my mouth, draining her body of its contents. When the car stops it's tumble, Elizabeth's screams cease.

Feeling full, I unlatch from her neck and wipe my face from the collected blood around my lips. Taking deep breaths, I finally see the damage that I've done. Elizabeth is pale and lifeless. She looks as if every inch of her soul had been drained out of her. Beside her, her husband is dead, his face is on the steering wheel. His eyes are still open, as they stare at me.

Looking at the older couple, I realize that I'm the reason why they're dead. They were such a nice couple and didn't deserve the deaths that I gave them. I hop out of the car in a daze and stare at my bloody hands.

I'm a murder.

I'm not too sure how long I sat outside the vehicle, but soon I heard a police siren in the distance. My gut tells me to run, but I feel responsible. I deserve what ever punishment comes to me.

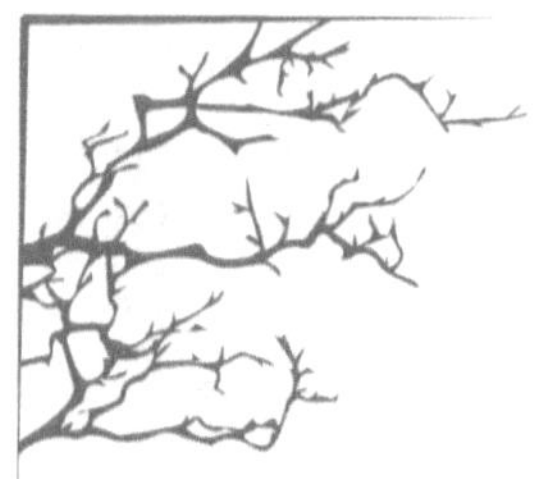

Chapter 5

Zane

Did I make the right choice letting her go? I've never heard of a vampling being permitted to be on their own. Yet I find myself breaking all types of rules for this woman. Why is that? What is wrong with me? What is captivating me to go out of my way for her. It feels like there is an invisible force, telling me that I should break every rule and kill every creature in her way to keep her safe. What is this feeling?

As I pace back in forth in my family's manor, I'm deep in thought until I feel an immense amount of fear. It over takes me and brings me to my knees.

"Hannah, she's in trouble."

Grabbing my phone, I start to dial her, but my phone buzzes indicating another call. Looking at the caller ID, see that it's , Adam, the local sheriff, which is never a good thing. Please don't let it be about Hannah.

"Hello?"

"Zane, I've got some bad news. There's been an unjust murder. We've found a rogue vampire."

"Was it Thomas?" I clinch my fist hoping that it isn't him. Since he's been exiled from our tribe, he's been causing us trouble as of late.

"No, it's a female. Blonde, upper twenties."

Hannah!

"I'll be right there."

Without another thought, I hang up the phone and sprint to my third story window. Leaping from the ledge, I transform into my bat and fly to the area Adam told me.

From my height above, I can see the two police cruisers blocking traffic, an ambulance and an overturned automobile. My heart races from the overview of the scene. Landing in the woods, I appear at the tree line to see Adam waiting for me. Behind him is Hannah, wrapped in a blanket, talking to a paramedic.

"What happened?"

"According to her, she was getting a ride to the city and the driver swerved to avoid a deer crashing his car into a tree."

I nod not believing a word of it.

"And what do you think happened?"

"Hannah, drained the old lady and killed the man before the car slammed into the tree. This vamp is clearly out of line. She has two unjust killings and should be punished. Should I detain her until your sister gets back from her visit with your father?"

"No, that's unnecessary. She's my mate."

"Your mate?" Adam gawks. He looks back at her then towards me. "I never knew you were querying for a human."

"Yeah, I did it in secret." I attempt to walk pass him towards Hannah. I really hope he doesn't ask me more questions.

"Regardless, she's an out of control vampling. Imagine if it was someone else who showed up to the scene of the crash first. I'm sorry, but I must report her to your father, Abdalla."

"Don't..." I growl, holding his arm.

"Unhand me." He snaps, glaring at me.

"Adam, listen we've known each other for over hundred years. I've never asked you of anything, but now I need your assistance. That woman over there is my mate. My true love." I lie, pointing at her.

"Taking her away will pain me. I'm not ready to part from her. You remember what it was like to be a vampling. That feeling of hunger driving you to do wrong. I remember when you were turned. It takes time. Please..."

Adam stares at me and then back at Hannah. Her eyes studies us. I know she could hear every word we speak and can sense my concern.

Adam scratches his chin and shakes his head.

"If Abdalla asks..."

"Lie. Tell them I was training her and things got out of hand. Her alibi is a good one. You and I both know that there's deer everywhere in these woods. Accidents can happen."

Adam nods. "I will cover for you."

"Thank you."

"...But no more slip ups. She kills again, I will report you both to Chief Abdalla. Understood?"

I nod and watch as Adam mumbles, walking away to talk to his other deputies.

I approach Hannah, who looks to be in shambles. I don't have to sense her emotions to know that she is sad and full of regret. I sit next to her on the ambulance and rub her back. She places her head on my shoulder and sighs.

"You were right. My old life is done. I didn't last one hour." She sobs. "Zane..it was all my fault. Those people didn't deserve to die like that."

I shush her and rub her back. "It's okay, Hannah. The important thing is your okay. You're right, those people didn't deserve to die, but let that be your first lesson. We are vampires. We will always be hungry. We will always want to kill. However, the difference between us and monsters is self-control. That is what defines us, without it we will be hunted and killed, either by our own kind or the humans. Understand?"

She nods and sniffs, wiping her tears away. "But I can't just vanish, without a trace. What about Ash?"

"Ash?"

"She's my best friend. We were supposed to go to brunch today. She's probably has the entire NYPD looking for me."

"If you are serious about leaving your old life behind, you can't contact her. Doing so will only open more questions."

"Zane...this is so much at once." She gasps.

"I know, but I will be there every step of the way."

"So what now?"

"Now, we train. We have three months to prepare for my father's arrival. We must convince him that we're in love."

"In love? Zane, I barely know you."

"I know, but we must. My father, he is the chief of this region's tribe. If he finds out that our mating is a sham, he will put us to death."

"Us? Your father will kill his own son?"

"Yes, he killed my younger brother for breaking the laws of our kind. I have no doubt he would do the same for us."

"Oh, Zane." Hannah rubs my arm and I stare into her eyes.

"I will not let that happen to us. I will protect you, but you must also play your part."

"As your wife?"

I nod. "Yes, for us to fool father we must act madly in love."

"Do you think he will fall for it?"

I shrug. "It's better than the alternative."

"So I must only be with you for all of eternity?"

I chuckle. "No, we don't have to be this way for the rest of our lives. There are some bonded vamp couples never that mate again after the turning. Vampires have been known to be polygamous with other humans."

"Well, that's a relief. How long do you suppose I could start dating?"

"Eh, give or take twenty years should be fine."

"Twenty years!"

I laugh again. "Ah, yes, my concept of time is a bit different than yours. Don't worry. Twenty years will past in no time."

Hannah cracks a smile. It is the first time I've seen her grin. It is as bright as the sun as she beams at me, and once more I am reminded of her beauty.

"Zane, you really have no concept of time do you?"

"No, I don't. I am sorry. I'm three hundred and twenty three, so time for me is relative. What is decades to you only feels like a small passage of time."

"You're three hundred and twenty three!"

I laugh and rub the back of my head. "Yes...is that a problem?"

"No, not at all. I always wanted to date an older mature man. I guess I got my wish."

"So we're dating now?"

"Eh..." she shrugs. "You're not half bad looking. I suppose I could give you a chance. Not to mention you did save my life. I owe you."

"You owe me nothing, Hannah."

She smiles at me, "You're a good guy, Zane."

"Thank you Hannah, are you ready to head home?"

"Yes, let's go."

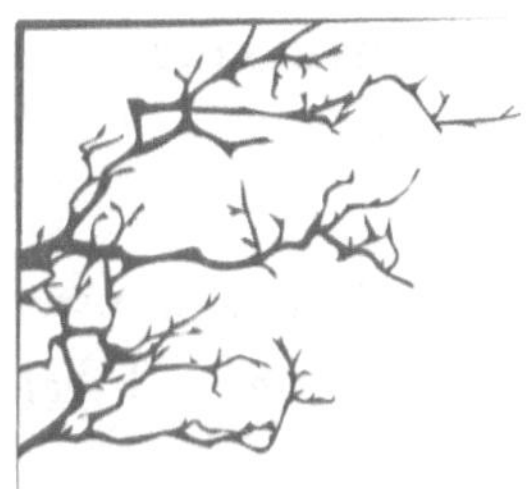

Chapter 6

Hannah

I wake up once more in the room I was in before. I have no idea what the time was, but I figure it was late afternoon as Zane and I didn't get back to the mansion until early morning. Walking towards the antique wooden dresser in the room, I find a handwritten note from Zane.

Good Afternoon Hannah,

I hope you slept well. Training will begin at six pm. Please feel free to take a shower. I have left out a towel and fresh clothes to change in. When you are ready, I will be in the dining room.

Zane

I smile at the handwritten note, and notice that Zane's handwriting reminds me of how someone would write with ink and quill. I laugh to myself imaging Zane writing the note out that way. I wouldn't put it past him as he's older than America itself.

As usual, the mansion is pitch black, but with my enhanced vision, I am able to navigate through the darkness with ease. The bathroom isn't to far from my room, and upon walking in, I see he left me a towel along with some athletic attire of a tank top and yoga pants.

Turning the shower on, I get in, cleaning my body from the remnants of last night. As the warm water pellets my face, visions of last night return to me. It all seems like a nightmare. I still remember what the old ladies blood tastes like. I can still hear her screams as I drain her of her life.

I killed her. I took her life. I am a murder.

Looking at my hands, my fingers began to tremble. Was I a monster for the things I've done? The longer I think about it, the worse I feel. Emotions wash over me and I fall in the shower crying.

I am not sure how long I cried, but I hear a soft tap on the bathroom door.

"Hannah? Are you okay?"

I sigh. "Yes, Zane I'm fine."

"Are you sure? I can feel your emotions right now. You're upset and sad. Is it about the woman you killed?"

"Yes, I feel terrible. I am a monster for murdering her."

"You are not a monster. You have a beautiful soul. I can tell, there's not an evil bone in your body."

"Yes, but that lady was an innocent. She was helping me, and I lost control."

"I know you did, but with training and time, it won't happen again. Consider that lesson number one. Let that be the last time you ever hurt an innocent. Use that memory as a motivator in your training. You're a strong, beautiful woman Hannah. I saw that the moment I laid eyes on you. You have a warriors spirit. You were pinned against that wall, the odds against you, yet you didn't blink. You stood tall and fought back. You're a fighter Hannah. I believe you can do this."

"You do?"

"Yes, Hannah, I do. I believe in you."

I smile hearing his reassurance. Zane's words fill me with hope, lighting up the darkness that is in my heart.

I take a deep breath and turn off the shower. After drying off, I get dressed and walk out of the bathroom. Zane is standing near the door when I exit.

"Thank you for being there."

Zane nods and his brown eyes peer into mine. "You're my mate. I will always be there."

His stare is bold and benevolent. His tender piercing gaze makes my heart flutter and I suddenly feel closer to him. The way that he said there, continues to ring in my head. His deep husky voice gives me shivers, and makes the hairs on my arm stand. I didn't know a lot about Zane, but I have a feeling that when he makes a promise he keeps it.

Avoiding his humble eyes, I cough and push an escaped strand of my hair behind my ear.

"So training?"

"Yes, are you ready?"

"As ready as I can be."

"Good. Come, you need to feed first."

I nod and follow him back into the dining room. Sitting down at the wooden table, I watch Zane pull out two bags of blood. He hands me one and holds on to the other.

"Blood type A is my favorite..."

"Really? What makes it so special?"

"The earthy tones in it. My least favorite is O. It's super bland."

I giggle. "I never thought I would be having a conversation about the way blood tastes. Have I gone insane?"

Zane chuckles, "No, I doubt it." He gives me a half smile, before ripping the bag and drinking it's contents.

I do the same. As soon as the metallic tasting liquid hits my tongue I moan, sipping the bag quickly. Blood ran down my cheeks as I squeezed every last drop in the bag.

"Someone's hungry. Would you like another one?"

"Sure, if you have it, I'll try some O positive."

"Oh, daring individual. I like it." He smirks. He grabs another two bags of blood from the fridge behind him and tosses one towards me. I scamper towards the bag and rip into it. As soon as the blood it's my lips, I detected the difference. Type A reminded me of savory baked chicken, while type O tasted like unseasoned ground beef.

"Oh, I see what your saying."

"Yeah, not as good right?" He finishes the bag and then tosses it into a nearby trash can.

"Yes, I think I will be sticking with Type A for here on out. That one tastes like chicken."

"Chicken?"

"Oh, I forgot. You never had chicken before have you?"

Zane shakes his head.

"It's amazing. My favorite is when it's fried. Oh, just thinking of the salty crunchy food is making my stomach rumble. So, you never even tried it?"

"I have, but like I said before, normal human foods doesn't quench our appetites. Only human blood."

"Oh, that's a shame. I was looking forward to a raw steak. So what is it like growing up as a vampire?"

"Being a young vampire is tough. It's difficult to survive as the hunger drives you. Good parents are needed to nurture the child, and keep their hunger at bay."

"Well, it sounds like your parents did a good job."

Zane scoffs and crosses his arms. He narrows his eyes as he glares at the table. "My parents were the farthest thing from perfect. My evil father would beat us to keep us in line, my mother wouldn't lift a finger to protect us. The brothers and sisters that my father saw as unfit were killed on the spot. I had ten siblings, and over the years, each one of them has been killed, just leaving my sister and me."

"Oh...Zane I'm sorry."

"It's okay. The life of a vampire is tough. We like to think ourselves as more advanced than humans, but in reality we're out of control savages. I mean who kills their own kin?"

"Humans do."

"Humans are not as barbaric as we are. You'll see. Perhaps it was unwise to turn you."

I give him a half smile, reach across the table, and rub his hand.

"Hey, you saved my life. For that I am grateful. Thank you."

His frown turns into a smile.

"You're welcome. Tell me, was your youth as competitive as mine?"

I giggle. "Never. Unless you count Saturdays during softball. Those games could be cutthroat."

"Ah, like the fighting pits?"

"Not quite. More like if you strike out and go 0-3 at bats, your parents won't talk to you the entire ride home."

"Oh, I don't understand the reference."

"It's okay. Just a bit of sports humor."

"Did you have a good childhood?"

"Well that's unfair, especially comparing my life to your story." I shrug, trying to remember the days of old. "my childhood was like a lot of kids in America. Went to school, went on summer vacations, got Christmas presents. That sort of thing."

"Sounds wonderful."

"Eh...it was pretty plain if you ask me."

"No, I wish my youth was like that. I made myself a promise that if I ever had kids, I wouldn't treat them harshly. I would love every single one of them."

"That's sweet."

"Do you want kids?" He asks. His eyes are focused on mine. Once more I feel his lingering bold stare, and once more I squirm from his gaze.

"With you?" I blurt.

Zane cracks a smile. "Well, we are mates. Like I said, we don't have to do anything you don't want to. I'm merely asking to get to know you."

"Oh..." I take a deep breath and clear my throat. "Well, I've thought about it once or twice. My ex and I had the same conversation."

"Was that your prior lover?"

"Yes, I should have left his ass years ago, but I stayed. Honestly, I don't know why, I guess I wanted to stick to the status quote. In the end, he cheated on me, putting that final nail in the coffin of our relationship."

"He cheated on you? How could a man do such a thing. A beauty such you, deserves to be treated like a queen. The traitor deserves to be killed. Would you like me to do it?"

I laugh. "And they say that chivalry is dead. No, I don't need you protecting my honor. That fucker will get what's coming to him eventually. I'm just glad I no longer have to deal with his bullshit. What about you Zane, do you have any skeletons in you closet?"

"Skeletons? Why would I keep the corpses of my victims?"

I giggle. "No, it's an expression. It's a phrase, a way of asking if you have any secrets or lovers in the past?"

"Oh, I see. No, not many. There was one human I was fond of. In 1910, there was a young teacher that worked in a school house nearby. Her name was Elizabeth." Just him saying her name a large smile spread on his face.

"She had smooth dark hair, soft porcelain skin, and a smile that would take your breath away. I met her when I was visiting the city. She used to sing nights at the downtown hotel. She had a beautiful voice. From that night I was smitten. We would meet at night at a hotel downtown. During our time together we would take long strolls through the park, have dinner and every night we shared a bed."

"Sounds romantic. Did you think about turning her?"

"I did, but my father didn't approve of it."

"Oh, I'm sorry."

"It's okay. Though I couldn't turn her, we still were madly in love with each other. I loved her until the day she died in 1956. Since then

I have not laid with a woman." Zane's voice falters as he looks at the table. I can tell that he is deep in thought. Reaching out, I grab his hand.

"You still care about her, don't you?"

"I do. That is my curse. To keep living even after my loved one had passed. I'd hope to have found a mate to love forever, but I have had no luck."

"That's how you were able to turn me?"

He nods. "I don't expect you to ever love me, Hannah. Let me be clear. You are free to love whom you want. Just know that I will always be your friend."

I grin, "as will I. You saved my life, it's the least I could do."

His frown breaks into a smile as he looks up from the table.

"Thank you, Hannah."

"Welcome," I grin. " Wow, what a romance for forty six years. Talk about a commitment. I wish my ex had your devotion."

"Commitment is easy when your in love."

"Ehh, I guess, until some pretty thang walks by you and catches your eye."

"No, then that's not love. That's lust."

"Yeah, I guess my ex and I were both in lust. So did you and Elizabeth ever have kids?"

"No, the procreation between vampire and human is impossible. I can only produce offspring with my vampire mate."

"Oh..." once more I feel the shame of Zane wasting his one chance to have children by turning me.

"Did you ever want kids?"

"Yes, I want to chance to give my kids the life I never had. My father, Abdalla, was rough and cold. I aim to be different than my father."

"That's nice of you." I finish the bag of O negative and place it on the table in front of me. Looking at Zane I snort.

"What's so funny?"

"Nothing."

"It's obviously funny. You can't stop laughing."

"Sorry, it's just that I can't imagine you as a little boy. You're more ripped than the Hulk, I just can't see how some scrawny kid became that man I see in front of me. Not to mention, you're over three hundred years old, how long did it take you to get to look like a twenty one year old man?"

"About two hundred years, give or take."

"Really? So will you always age until you become an old man and die?"

"Vampires are immoral. Through the years our bodies will mature, but we stop growing when we would look like a human who is aged fifty."

"Well, that's nice to know. Will the effects be the same with me?"

"Yes, as soon as you turned, your body was affected. As long as you keep drinking blood, you will live for eternity."

I whistle. "Well, damn. I bet your 401k looks amazing."

"I don't understand. Is that a joke?"

"You know, since you're living forever, you can invest and..."

Zane and I share a look and I laugh once more.

"You know what, that was a bad joke. I'm pretty sure you don't even have investments."

"I have gold. Does that count?"

I chuckle. "Yeah, something like that. You really need to get out more."

"I do. I fly over the city every night."

"That's not what I mean." I smirk at his awkwardness. "Speaking of flying, when do I get to turn into a bat?"

"Soon, that however is the most difficult thing a vampire can do. Like a child you must learn to walk before you can run. Come. Let's train."

I nod and follow him outside. Leaving the mansion, I could feel the gentle breeze on my back as we look at the vast dark forest. Above us, the moon and stars are our only light during early night. In the backyard, the mansion was on top of a hill, and fifty feet below is a valley covered in trees. Zane walks towards the courtyard's balcony

"What's the first lesson?" I ask.

"Follow me." He jumps off the third story balcony, and lands below with a hard thud. "Come on!"

"Umm? Are there stairs?"

"You won't break your bones. Trust me. They are as hard as stone. The fall won't kill you. Trust me."

I breathe and look down. Already I could feel the nausea from the tall distance. "This was crazy..." I shake my head. "What is wrong with me?"

"Just jump, Hannah. It will be okay. Trust me." Zane shouts.

I close my eyes and hop on the ledge. Standing there, I shake my head. "This is crazy."

"Hannah, jump!"

"Fuck it." I didn't think as I leap forward. I am airborne, and for a mere second I feel like I am flying before I crash down to earth.

"Oh, shit!" I scream as I tumble to the ground. My landing isn't graceful at all as I land on my back. However, I don't feel a thing as I roll on the ground.

"You see, easy."

"Yeah sure. How was my landing?"

Zane smirks. "It needs work, but you'll get the hang of it. Come on, follow me!"

He moves in a blur across the forest. I have to blink twice at his super human speed. He moves like the Flash, dashing across the forest like lighting.

"Keep up!" He yells from a distance.

"I can't even see you!"

"You can smell me though, right?"

"Smell? Zane I can't..." before I can get the words out, his scent catches my nose. At first I think my senses are playing tricks on me until I remember what Zane's earthy tones smell like. His masculine scent makes my stomach flutter and my knees quake. I breathe attempting to keep my basic urges at bay as I suddenly feel attracted to him.

Closing my eyes, I focus and I am able to trace out his location. Once I find him, I open my eyes and take off running. Pumping my legs, I notice that I am moving at a inhuman fast pace. Trees are blurring past me as I run. My jaw drops at my incredible speed.

How am I moving so fast?

I lose focus for one second, and that is all it takes for me to lose my footing and trip. I face plant hard into the ground, and slide across the forest floor.

When I come to, I see Zane standing above me with a smirk on his face.

"Are you okay?"

"Peachy." I growl, dusting myself off. "Everything hurts right now."

"Well, you did just trip running two hundred miles per hour, It's going to feel horrible if you fall."

"Two hundred miles..." my jaw drops.

Zane laughs. "Yes, as vampires we are blessed with superhuman strength and speed. Now come. Follow me."

I nod and chase after Zane. He is much faster than me as I attempt to keep up. He zigzags through trees, leap over logs and streams, and able to climb tall mountains, all making following him a brutal task. I have no idea if I am even in the state of New York anymore.

When we finally stop, I gasp, placing my hands on my knees. We were in a wide open space with trees all around us. In front of me is an open space with a circle made of small white rocks. To the left are multiple large boulders that appears to been placed there, and to my right is a rock structure that is in a shape of a human.

"Welcome to West Virginia." Zane grins.

"West Virginia!" I gawk.

Zane laughs at my expression. "Yes, you just ran over five hundred miles."

"That's impossible..."

"Super human speed, remember?"

I nod. "Where are we?"

"These are the training grounds I used as I child. Everyday, we will run here to train. Our objective is to get you ready for my father's homecoming. No doubt my father will test you, since you haven't properly been vetted as a human. He will want to see your strength on full display. He will want to make sure, you are able to use your full abilities, and if you can't, he will not hesitate to kill us both."

"So what must I do?"

"I believe that father will want you see you be able to top speeds of over three hundred miles per hour, he will want to make sure that you're an adequate fighter, and lastly you must be able to turn into a bat. With that I mind, we will run to this spot every day until you can get here under two hours, I will also teach you hand to hand combat. Lastly when your ready you will learn to transform into a bat."

"Why can't I do that now?"

"Transforming into a bat is one of the hardest things for a vampire to do. It requires focus and discipline. It takes years for a vampling to learn this, but you only have three months until my father gets here."

"Okay, what's first?"

"We spar. I must learn of your combat abilities."

"I have no idea how to fight."

"You showed promise in the alley. Just hit me and we will go from there."

I nod and ball my fist. I attempt to strike Zane, but he dodges my attack easily.

"Come on, Hannah hit me."

"I'm trying."

"There's no trying! If someone decides to attack, you must be able to defend yourself. Come on! Hit me!"

I growl and attempt to hit him. With every punch, he dodges my strikes with ease. I over extend on one punch and he ducks underneath and delivers a powerful haymaker to my face. The punch upends me, and I twist and the air, landing hard on the ground. I groan in pain as my face stings from his hard attack. Blood drips from my chin, and my jaw feels like it's been hit by a truck.

Zane didn't say a word at me. His eyes are cold and rough. He walks away from me, turning his back. "Get up Hannah."

"Zane...just get me a second."

"No, get up!" He roars, his eyes narrows, glaring at me. "You will not be given any mercy if you have to fight my sister. It is life or death in the fighting pits. There is no in between. There is no mercy. You must be able to fight back or you will die. I will not lose you. Now, *get up!*"

I sigh and dust myself off. I can feel the blood roll down my cheek from Zane's punch. I put my fist up and ignore the pain as I attempt to strike Zane again.

Anger fuels my attacks. I roar as I blindly swing at him. Once more he dodges my attack. This time he hits my face with a quick one two combo, and before I could regroup, he knees me hard in the stomach. I gasp as it feels like his entire knee is going through my body. I double over falling into the ground clutching my stomach. Tears roll down my cheeks from the pain.

Zane towers over me. He shows no remorse. "Get up Hannah..."

"Zane I can't..." I cry.

"I won't take no for an answer. You enemy will not pause. They will not stop for you. They will kill you. You must be strong. I believe in you, Hannah. You have a the will. You have the strength. I've seen it when you fought off those men in the alley. Don't give in. Remember what I said earlier about those people you killed. Don't let their deaths be in vain. If you can't do it for yourself, do it for them. Pay respects to them by training now, and becoming the strongest vampire you can so that next time, you won't kill an innocent when you lose control. You must fight. You must be strong. I believe in you. Now get up."

I breath deeply, spit out some blood, and slowly stand. Every inch of my body is in pain as I place my hands up to defend myself. I want to quit, but my mind keeps replaying the accident. I keep visioning the old woman's drained body. I keep hearing her screams.

Zane is right, if I don't want to be the monster, I have to be in control. I have to fight.

My fists clench, as I feel renewed. A smirk spreads on my face as my eyes focus on Zane.

"I'm ready."

"Good, now hit me."

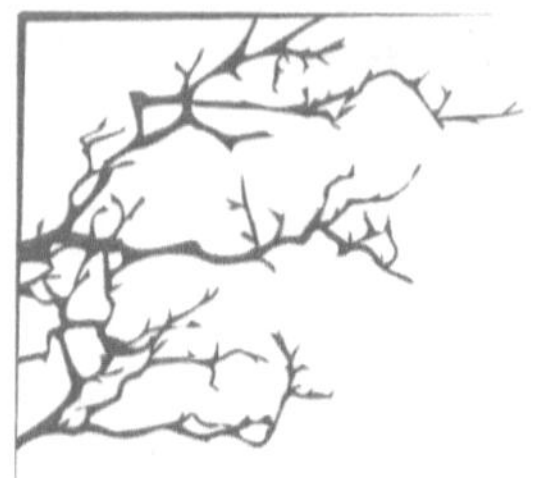

Chapter 7

Zane

"**A**gain!" I yell.

Hannah yells and lifts the large rock off the ground to toss it a few feet. Above our heads, a quarter moon gives us limited light, but, we don't need it as our eyes are sharp in the dark.

We've been at the training ground since dusk and she has yet to show fatigue. I am impressed with her perseverance, but I know the real test is months away. She's still not ready for the trials that my father will put her through. Thus I must push her beyond her normal limits. She must be ready.

"Good job. Again!"

She walks towards another large rock and tosses it to the same location as the other. Hannah is wearing only a tank top and yoga pants. Her blonde hair is tied in a ponytail, and sweat drips down her pale skin.

Like her, I'm wearing a white sleeveless top, with a pair of black shorts. My eyes are focusing on her every move.

"Very good. Again!"

She breathes deeply before grabbing another rock and tossing it the same distance. Watching her, a small smile curls on my face as I watch her progress. Over the last month, she has improved exponentially. We are now able to get to West Virginia under two hours, and she has shown the ability to use her strength.

Physically, her body has shown changes as well, as her muscles are more defined than before. While her fighting skills are still under par, she has impressed me as of late. The other day, I actually had to block several punches, instead of dodging them.

When the last rock in her row is thrown, Hannah places her hands on her hips and takes long winded breaths. Despite the extra bags of blood, the intense training appears to be taking a toll on her as her pale skin was covered in bruises.

"How was that?" She asks.

"Good. Your speed and strength are improving. Let's spar."

She nods and gets into a fighting stance. I do the same as I wait for her attack.

"Begin!" I growl.

She yells and attacks me quickly. I dodge the first two attacks, but with every strike she gets closer and closer. On her last punch, I barely have enough time to react, and I have to place my hands above my face to protect me. After punching my block, she swiftly crouches and sweeps my leg, tripping me. I fall to the ground, and before I had a chance to recover, she is on top punching me. I place both arms up blocking her attacks, before I shove her away.

She rolls on the ground and I flip up to my feet.

"Good."

"I landed a strike on you." She smirks.

"Don't get cocky. Again."

Filled with confidence, Hannah attacks me again. I can't help but to smile at our sparing session. She has come along so much since that first day we fought. It is actually a challenge having to block her punches and kicks. She attacks with such power that it knocks me off balance. Her defensive skills are vastly improving too, as she is able to block my own attacks.

We trade blows back and forth for a few minutes before she finally punches me square in the jaw. I step back and rub my chin.

"Oh, did I get you there?" She mocks.

I spit out some blood and grin. "Again."

Hannah laughs and charges at me. She punches me twice and does a high kick. I dodge the attacks and attempt to punch her. She blocks and tries to deliver a haymaker. I block it and place her in a arm bar, pulling her close towards me. Holding her tightly, I smell her feminine musk and her sweetness makes my body flutter. I try to compose myself, but the smell drives me mad.

Hannah breaks free of my hold and regroups. We circle each other, both of us grinning as we look into each other eyes.

"Are you getting worse at this?" She quips

"Or are you getting better?" I wink.

"Touché."

Hannah attacks me again. I block her advance and punch her in the stomach. She retaliates with a severe blow to my head. I stumble back and toss her over my hip. On the ground, I attempt to kick her but she rolls away. She flips on her feet, and charges at me. She swaps between punching and kicking. Her furry of attacks leave me in defense mode. I am unable to counter as I retreat backwards.

I over extend and she punishes me for my mistake, placing me in an arm bar, tripping me, and finishing me with a hard punch in my sternum. She raise her fist again preparing another blow.

"Hannah stop!"

She hesitates and I used the opportunity to grab her arm and flip her over me. I punch her hard in stomach and stand back up.

"Hey!" She growls, slapping the ground. "I won that fight. That was a dirty move."

"Never allow mercy. If you do, your enemy will always use that against you."

She chuckles. "You always have to make a lesson out of something."

"It's the only way you can learn."

"Some teacher you are," she smirks. "Are you ready for round two?"

"Always..." I grin, getting in my fighting stance.

Hannah comes at me again and once more I trade blows with her. As we fight our eyes kept connecting. It isn't an angry glare or a stare to guess our next move, it is a flirtatious gaze as if we are both admiring each other. I didn't have to sense her feelings to know that something is growing between us. I feel the same way she feels. Over the last month, there has been an indescribable force pulling us together. The more we spend time with each other the closer I feel to her.

With both hands, I push her back, and she opens her eyes wide from my assault, she attempts to counter, but before she could, I transform into my bat, and duck underneath her arms. I fly around her and transform again. By the time she can regroup, my arms were already around her to hip toss her.

She rolls across the ground. She pops up and dusts herself off.

"Damn! What a move. That was awesome."

"Thanks," I grin.

"Now, you have to teach me to transform into a bat."

I shake my head. "You're not ready. Transforming is difficult."

"I know it is, but it's been a month. You haven't even explained how to do it."

I sigh. "Okay, sit down, I'll explain."

She nods and sat on a nearby rock.

"Transforming not only takes practice but will as well. You must have the want to do it."

"I want to..."

I hold up my hand. "I know you do, but it's more that than. It's a need. Most vampires only change the first time when they are distressed, when they feel their backs are up against the corner they awaken the transformation inside them. The easiest way is for a vampling to be beaten into a submission. That's how I learned."

"Is that what your going to do to me?"

I shake my head. "No, perhaps if I were my father I would, but I do not want to go that path."

"So how will I transform?"

"I want you to meditate."

"Really?"

"Yes, close your eyes, attempt to reach out to the bat."

"Umm okay..." she closes her eyes. I stand watching her. Twenty minutes later, her eyes open.

"Yeah, I'm not feeling nothing."

"Keep trying. It's there. Trust me. Just reach out."

"Zane, this is crazy. I mean...Isn't there another way?"

"Besides distress? No, and I will not beat you into submission. I won't treat you the way my family treated me."

"They really did a number on you didn't they?"

I nod, my body reflexively flinches as horrible memories of my past resurface.

"Hey..." Hannah softly replies. She gets off the ground and holds my hand. Her hands in mine feels warm. My body stirs from her embrace. Her eyes look into mine as she slowly gets closer to me. I feel her arms wrap around my back as she gives me a gentle hug. I close my eyes, enjoying her closeness. I can't explain why but having her hold me washes away the fear I have.

"It's okay. You're nothing like you're family. I don't know much about them, but I do know that you're a good man. You could've left me to die in that alleyway, but you didn't. You could have beaten me into submission but you didn't. You care for me, just like I care for you."

"Thank you, Hannah."

She smiles at me and gives me another big hug. I grin rubbing her back as I realize that Hannah and I are closer than I thought.

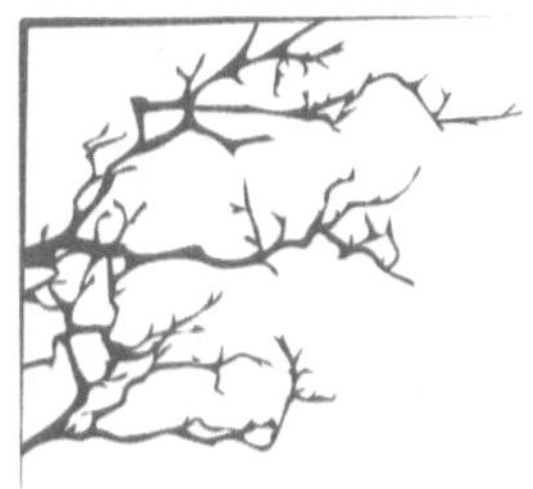

Chapter 8

Hannah

Walking into the gym, I find Zane working out. He is on his back, bench pressing five tons. I can't help but to ogle his physique.

He is shirtless, with only a pair of grey sweats on. His dark skin is glistening with sweat, and his buff chest is well defined. My eyes drift lower toward his core and observe his washboard abs clench every time he lifts the bar.

My stomach stirs as my vision focuses on his distinct bulge in his sweats. Even in the darkness, I could make out his large member outlined in his baggy sweatpants. My body shivers as I am overwhelmed by my sudden lust.

What is going on with me?

I hover watching him until he clears his throat. "You know it's rude to stare."

"Oh..." I rub my arm after being caught. "Sorry, I was just impressed with the amount of weights you were lifting."

"Would you like to try?"

"That? I'm not even sure I could lift the bar."

"I'm sure you can. I believe in you. Come and try."

I raise my eyebrows and walk into the small gym. Zane gets up, wipes the bench off, and then allows me to lay down.

On my back I'm looking up at him. My focus should be on lifting, yet I am drawn towards his sexy exterior. Once more, my eyes are glued to his sculpted frame. Once more, my eyes drift below his waist, and once more my body squirms at the sight.

"Are you ready?" He asks, breaking me of my spell.

"Yes," I breathe.

He nods and places his hands underneath the bar to spot me. I take a deep breath and lift the bar, to my surprise I am able to move it.

"Take it slow," he instructs.

I breathe slowly, lowering the bar towards me. Once it hits my chest, I push, and I could feel my arms struggling with the weight.

"You got this Hannah. Push, push push!" He encourages.

I roar as I push the weight. I gave it my all and my body shakes from the exertion.

"Come on Hannah you're almost there! I believe in you!"

Zane's faith in my gives me the added boost I need. I grit my teeth and scream as I push the bar back onto the rack.

"You did it!" He grins.

"Thanks. I can't believe I just benched five thousand pounds. I feel like a freaking superhero."

Zane chuckles. "Yes, it's very impressive."

"After all that lifting I'm starving. Care to join me in the dining room for a pint of A positive blood?"

"Normally, I would, but I think you are ready for your first kill."

"Zane, I can't. You know that I'm still recovering from the last time I killed someone."

"Hannah, you are a vampire. You must eat, and you won't always be able to drink hospital blood."

"Yes, but I'm murdering someone."

"Tell me, do you have your own self doubts when you eat a steak from a cow?"

"Zane, that's different."

"Is it though? You are killing an innocent animal for nutrients. That is no different than what we are doing."

"True, but humans are different?"

"How so? I think humans are worse than the animals they kill. They are destructive and hostile towards their own kind. They have no disregard on how they kill other things. In my eyes, humans are equally monsters as we are."

"Yes, but not all humans are monsters. There are good people in this world."

"Yes, we know. That is why we only go after the lowest of the low. The scum of the earth. That is who we choose to feed on."

"Like drug dealers, murders, and rapists?"

"Yes, those people deserve death. That is why we go after them."

"Well, I guess that's not too bad…"

Zane nods. "The sheriff, you met earlier. He is one of us. He provides us with inside information on who we should feed on. He just gave me a tip on someone downtown. Would you like to accompany me?"

I am concern about killing another human, but Zane is right. Killing a criminal that deserves death eases my conscience.

"Yes, if I must."

"Good. Get dressed. We go on the hunt in an hour."

We leave the gym and go to our respected rooms to put on our street attire. I change into a pair of black leather leggings, along with a dark corset top. I wrap my hair into a bun and smile at my appearance in the mirror. Over the last two months, I would have never expected to wear what I'm wearing. I've never been one for the black gothic look, but seeing as I'm a vampire now, it is time to go with the cliché style.

Taking a deep breath, I exit my room, and find Zane waiting for me.

His own attire matches my own goth style of leather pants, black shirt and a leather trench coat.

"You look lovely. Ready for your first hunt?"

"About as ready as I ever will be."

Zane nods. "Follow me."

I walk down the hallway beside Zane.

"How are we getting to downtown? Are we running or something?"

Zane chuckles. "No, running there would draw to much attention. We drive in style."

"Drive? You own a car?"

"Several. Come on." He leads me outside to a separate building of the mansion.

Reaching in his pocket he brings out a remote and clicks a button. I hear a garage door opening, and a black 69' SS Camaro is sitting in the garage.

"Oh, my! How do I not know about this?"

Zane shrugs. "You never explored the mansion's grounds?"

"No, I mean, I thought this building was where you guys harvested blood or something?"

Zane chuckles. "I told you, we have skeletons in our closets."

I giggle and hold my side.

"What?"

"Nothing. You're using that phrase wrong again."

He smirks at me and follows me into the garage.

"Wow, this car is amazing." I slide my hand across the smooth glossy black hood. I inspect the car, appreciating the sleek finish of the classic. "It's in pristine condition."

"Yes, it's one of my favorites."

"Mine too. I always wanted a sports car. Specifically a SS Camaro."

"Really?"

"Yeah, but living in NYC you don't really need a car, so it never made any sense."

"Ah, I see." Zane looks at his keys before tossing them to me.

"Zane? What was that for?"

"Your driving."

"I'm driving?"

"Yes, you're driving your car."

"*Your* car? Wait are you giving this to me?"

Zane chuckles. "That is what a gift is, unless the term gift means something else now."

"No! It's the same. Oh Zane! Wow, thank you!" I leap into his arms and give him a big hug. We remain in a tight embrace until I lean back and look into his brown eyes. Once more I feel a shiver up my spine. The way he admires me makes me feel like I'm the only woman in the world. I am not used to that.

My ex's eyes were always scanning, always looking at other women behind my back, but Zane is different as his stare penetrates my soul, making me feel things that I thought were impossible.

After a lingering embrace, we break and Zane clears his throat.

"Are you ready to go?"

"Yes, let's get out of here."

He nods and gets into the passenger side, I hop into the drivers side and turn the car over. The engine purrs to life and rumbles the steering wheel. I couldn't help but to smile from the powerful feeling. Pressing down on the accelerator, I zoom out of the mansion towards downtown.

I could feel Zane's eyes on me as I turn onto the highway.

"You know staring is rude."

"Sorry, I was just checking. You seem nervous."

"Is it that obvious?"

"Yes, I don't even have to detect your emotions. I can see it. You're gripping the steering wheel tightly and I can sense that you're at unease. Your first kill is always be the hardest. You will be fine."

"Will I?"

"Yes, it won't be like last time. I promise."

I nod. "Do you remember your first hunt?"

"Yes, it was a lot different than this. I was fifteen years old, and I heard of a rapist that was terrorizing a village nearby. I tracked him, caught him and killed him on the spot. There's nothing like your first hunt. The thrill of the chase and the taste of the warm blood is second to none."

"Any regrets?"

Zane shakes his head. "None. Not once have I ever regretted my decisions. These criminals that we kill deserve their gruesome deaths."

"Do they? I mean what makes us judge, jury, and executioner?"

"They broke the law, they deserve what's coming to them."

"So you're telling me that this drug dealer deserves to die? What if he has a family. He will be missed."

Zane shakes his head. "This man that we're going after is a menace. He's been locked up multiple times, but the legal system fails and he's always back on the street. We are doing society a favor. This man has more blood on his hands than we do. He's a murder, and distributes drugs to minors and others. He's scum."

"Well, I guess that makes me feel a little better."

"Good, now take this next left. His last known location is down this street."

I nod and turn down the road. We park the car two blocks away and walk to a townhouse. The home looks to be in shambles and it is obvious it's drug house. Sitting on the stoop in front are three men chatting. Leaning close to me, Zane whispers, "you see the man in the middle?"

"Yeah,"

"That's your mark. Find a way to get him down the alley."

I nod and approach the rough looking drug dealer.

"Hi, I want some drugs." I blurt towards the man.

Zane cracks a smile as if he's holding back a laugh. Perhaps I shouldn't have been so blunt, but I've never bought drugs before so I have no idea how to order anything.

The dealer laughs. "Yo, you're in the wrong neighborhood. Comic con is at the convention center. Get lost before something bad happens. I'm doing you a favor."

Zane raises his eyebrows and looks back at me.

I clear my throat and shake my head. "No, I was told you're the man to talk to about getting coke. I want a bag of it."

The dealer laughs again. "Yo are you a cop? You're acting like a narc."

"I'm not a narc. Trust me. I'm just a rich blonde white girl looking to get high."

The dealer smacks his lips and looks at his friends.

"A'ight Trinity. I hear yah. You want to take the red pill and head to Wonderland. I got you. Let's get you out of the Matrix." He jokes. "Morpheus you want something to?"

"No, it's just for her." Zane replies.

He nods his head looks towards me. "One hundred."

I pause realizing that I had no money, but Zane is a step ahead of me, handing the dealer the cash. The dealer counts the money before nodding towards his friend. The friend to his left, opens his jacket and hands me the cocaine.

"Now get lost." The dealer growls, looking away.

Zane looks at me, reminding me that I was supposed to get him towards the alley.

"Wait, I want something else. You got ex?

"You really want to party, huh? It's another hundred."

Zane cocks an eye at me, I could tell he was wondering what I was doing.

"Hundred? That was all the money we had." I lie. Honestly I didn't even know if Zane had the money, but my mind is on something more sinister.

"Well, there's other ways of payment," he smirks.

Perfect. He's a creep.

I think Zane understood my plan and plays his part too. "What did you have in mind?" Zane asks.

The dealer chuckles, "well judging by your leather, I can tell your lady is a freak. How about her and I go around the alley, and we make a deal in the oldest form of payment."

"My thoughts exactly." I reply, batting my eyes.

"Yo, I'll be right back." The dealer snickers as I take his hand and lead him away.

Zane follows, but the dealer places his hand on Zane's chest.

"Yo, this isn't a party. You chill here. Trust me I'll be gentle with your snow bunny."

"Zane, it's fine." I reply.

Zane nods and watches me walk hand in hand with the dealer. Walking away, I can detect a strong envious emotion going through me. It's strange that I am feeling jealous until I realize that the emotion isn't mine, but Zane's. It was powerful and breathtaking.

Is he jealous of me flirting with the dealer?

I look back and I could see Zane's jaw clinch and his fist balled. While I know we're not serious together, it is nice to feel his concern and jealousy over me leaving with the dealer.

I turn and give him a wink and a smile, attempting to keep him at ease. He gives me a small wave, but his eyes remains glued to the dealer.

The dealer and I turn the corner, and my hands start to tremble knowing the act I was going to perform.

"So, how did you want to pay for this, ma?"

"I have a few ideas," I push him against her wall and kiss him. He moans as he shoves his tongue in my mouth.

Yuck.

Kissing him, I hear his heartbeat, causing my blood lust to increase. I break away from his lips and kiss his neck. I lick his skin, and his masculine scent is driving my hunger.

"Yeah baby. I knew you were a freak," I hear him moan, groping my ass. I didn't let it bother me. I have him where I want him.

Second later, I grow my fangs and sink my teeth into his skin.

"What the fuck!" He yells, flailing against me. I'm only able to take a few sips of him before he pushes me away. His eyes are wide, glaring at me.

"You, bitch!" He growls. Blood running down his neck, he reaches behind his back for his gun. As soon as I see it, I'm attacking him.

He only fires once, but I am fast enough to dodge the bullet. I knock his gun out of his hands.

"Bitch!" He growls.

The fool didn't recognize that he was outmatched. I use that to my advantage. He attempts to punch me, but I block him. I push his arm away, and hit him with a one two combo in his face. I draw blood.

As soon as I see it, I tackle him to the ground. I pin him down and make my move. Sinking my teeth in, I groan as his warm blood tastes sweeter than sugar.

Drinking from him, I am not aware of my surroundings as I hear a shot ring out.I am too slow to react as I feel a stinging pain in my arm.

"Get her!" The dealer weakly screams.

The goon attempts to fire at me again, but I dodged his second attack. I charge at him, but Zane is quicker than me as he attacks the man from behind. With one hand, he lifts up the man by his neck.

"No one shoots at my mate." He growls before snapping his neck.

The man falls lifeless to the ground.

"Hannah, are you okay?"

"I'm fine." I reply.

He smiles at me, and I return the gesture until I notice five more guys in the alleyway.

"Zane, behind you!"

Zane turns and growls attacking the man nearest to him. I roar as I join the fray. I perform a double kick to a man's torso and then punch him hard in the stomach. I feel my fist go through his body and blood coating my hand. I watch as the life drains from his eyes as he falls to the ground.

I didn't think, as I am fighting two men. Blocking and dodging their attacks, I used the instructions that Zane taught me and use their attacks to my advantage. When I see my opening, I counter killing both men with ease.

As I get covered by their blood, I didn't once think about my prior hesitations. I didn't worry about if they had a family or if they did a thing bad in the past. I didn't care. All I care about is protecting Zane, and I can tell Zane has the same thoughts.

I'm not sure how many we killed, but they just kept coming at us. Zane and I stood back to back, ripping through our multiple attackers, and dodging bullets, knifes and fists as if we are a dynamic duo from a comic book. We are brutal in our attacks, killing any man that got near.

When we are through, bodies of our slain lay everywhere. Zane turns and looks at me, smiling. His face is drenched with blood. His evil smile is dark and twisted, I should be frightened by his demonic posture, but instead I am turned on by it. I'm turned on by his muscular sexy body dripping in blood. I'm turned on by his soulless black eyes, and by his sharp fangs stained by crimson blood.

I don't know what is wrong with me. I murdered dozens of people yet, I feel no remorse. I feel like a God stomping on ants.Perhaps it's the blood lust, perhaps it was the thrill of the fight, or it could just simplify be the fact that I find Zane incredibly sexy. Right there I wanted to kiss him, but I decide against it. Instead, I give him a toothy grin.

"Well, dig in." He winks, getting his knees to drain his first victim.

I did the same draining the body of his remaining blood. Three months ago I would've have been disgusted with myself, now I couldn't be more proud.

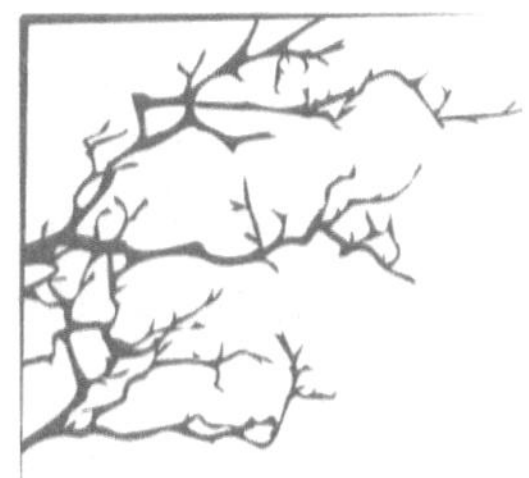

Chapter 9

Zane

I can't stop smiling at Hannah. Damn did she look sexy covered in blood. Between the crimson stains on her pale skin, her tight leather pants fitting her curvy thighs, and the corset top that made her breasts look twice as big, I am smitten. I can't take my eyes off her. Nor can she as her sexy blue eyes keep peering into my own.

I can sense her lust. She is full of it like me. It's overwhelming. It's a throbbing sensation that can only be cured by one thing. Sex.

I can't take my eyes off her, entering the mansion. Her presence is intoxicating, blinding my senses. All I want is her.

"What a rush!" She giggles with glee, opening the door.

"You were amazing out there."

"So we're you." She smirks.

I take a step closer to her. Our eyes connect. There's tension in the air as neither of us move. We linger in each other's presence, slowly inching towards each other.

"Zane?"

"Yes..." I breathe. My fingers twitch from our shared electricity. There is no denying that we are sharing a special spark.

"What am I feeling right now?"

"You are feeling my emotions."

"Really?"

"Yes."

"And right now..." she hesitates, her eyes scanning mine. Her lip quivers. I bite my own as at the moment all I want to do is feel her skin slide across my own. I want to taste her lips, and hear her moan as I'm buried deep inside her.

"...I I feel a burning desire." She mutters, batting her eyes. "Are your thoughts true?"

Before I can get answer out I hear my father's booming voice.

"Zane!"

My eyes open wide, as I turn to find my father with my sister. Like Oye, my father, Abdalla, is in his formal robes. He is always one for tradition.

"It appears that we caught you at an bad time?" He smirks.

"Not at all." I turn and straighten my jacket. Hannah looks at me and then towards my father.

My father's eyes didn't leave Hannah's as he studies her.

"So, this is your chosen mate?"

"Yes, father."

"Strange, I didn't know you were dating a human at the time."

"Father, I'm sorry to not inform you earlier, however Hannah and I are in love."

"Is that so?"

"Er, yes sir." Hannah adds. "Zane is the love of my life."

Abdalla stares at Hannah before clearing his throat. "Huh, regardless, you didn't follow the law. It takes years to seek approval to turn a mate, yet you did it behind my back."

Hannah and I share an anxious stare.

"Yes, father. I'm sorry. It's just that Hannah and I are in love and..."

"Love? What would you know of love? You speak of it as if you've been alive for a millennia. Tell me, how did you two meet?"

I didn't know what to say as suddenly my mouth felt heavy.

"We met at a bar. Zane and I were captured by each other as soon as he said hello." Hannah lies.

My father raises his eyebrows. "Is that so?"

"Yes, Hannah and I have been dating for over two years. Only a year ago did I tell her my true self. Oye has known about this."

My sister shakes her head at me, knowing that I just tied her to my lie. My father turns to my sister.

"Did you know?"

"Yes, I was aware." She lies. My sister's eyes narrows at me. "Yet, I advised *against* turning her without the approval of the tribe's chief."

My father nods. His eyes never leave Hannah's.

"No matter how much you love her, she still hasn't faced the trials nor has she gained my approval. This was an unsanctioned turn. I can't let disorder run in my own household."

"Father..." I step forward, but my father's glare turns towards me.

"Don't you dare! You've already caused enough trouble as it is. Hannah, is an unsanctioned turn, she will face a trial of combat."

"Father no!" I growl.

However, my father doesn't flinch at my plea. "The fight will be to the death. Hannah, if you kill my champion, you can remain in your position."

"Hannah..." I turn towards her. My eyes peer into her own, begging her not to accept. "There is another way. Please don't accept this!"

"I accept." She replies with her eyes narrow with determination.

I close my eyes as she accepts her doomed fate.

"Who is the champion that I must fight?"

"Oye..." my father grins, knowing that Oye is the most skilled fighter in North America.

Hannah stands in shock as she looks at Oye and towards me. I can see the realization dawned on her. She looks towards me and I can feel her fear. It overwhelms me. My fists clench and I didn't think, I just acted.

"Hannah, run!" I shout as I catch my sister off guard punching her.

"Brother!" She shouts.

"I will not let you harm her!" I punch her again.

"This is foolish! Stop this madness!" She blocks my second punch and attempts to punch me.

"No, she's my mate. To harm her is to harm me."

"Is this your choice?" She asks. I can see her hesitation.

"Yes," I reply.

Oye closes her eyes as if my decision is a knife to the chest. "Then I will do what I must." She headbutts me hard and I stumble back. I growl and charge at her. My sister and I trade blows. Each attack pains me. I didn't want to fight my sister, but to keep Hannah safe, I will do it.

From the corner of my eye, I watch Hannah leaving the estate. Behind her, my father attempts to go after Hannah, but I am quicker. With the thought of losing Hannah flowing through me, I feel more powerful than normal.

With a powerful haymaker I bring my sister to her knees. She attempts to regroup, but I'm quicker, knocking her out with a hard kick.

I chase my father down the hall and tackle him from behind. On top of him, I pummel him with a fury of punches. With every punch he feels my rage. How dare he threaten her.

He doesn't get a chance to lay a finger on me. I don't give him that chance.

With one more final punch, I knock him out cold. Standing up I look at the bodies of my family realizing what I've done. There is no going back after what I did, but I didn't care. It is all for Hannah. She needs me. She's my mate, and regardless of how we feel about each other, I didn't want her to be executed.

I take one last look before, I ran out of the house. Leaving the building, I jump into the air and transform into my bat to catch Hannah.

With her fast speed, she is already miles away from the house before I catch her. I fly ahead of her and transform, landing in front of her.

"Zane," she shrieks. Her arms hug me and she rubs my back.

"Are you okay?" I ask.

"Yes, but is your father serious? Was he really going to put me to death?"

I nod. "I couldn't let that happen. I've attacked my sister and father. They will not let that stand. They will be after us."

"What do we do?"

"We hide. We will stay on the run. We stay one step ahead of them and we will survive."

"I can't let you just throw away everything for me."

I grab her pale face cheeks and stare into her eyes. "Hannah you are my mate. No matter how you feel about me, this will never change. I will fight anyone who stands in our way to keep you safe. A mates bond is the strongest bond between vampires. I will not lose you. Understand?"

I could feel her body tremble as her blue eyes linger on mine.

"I understand." She whispers.

"Good, now, we need to put as much distance between us and New York. Come, it's only a matter of time before my family awakens from their unconscious, and when they do, we will have the entire vampire nation looking for us."

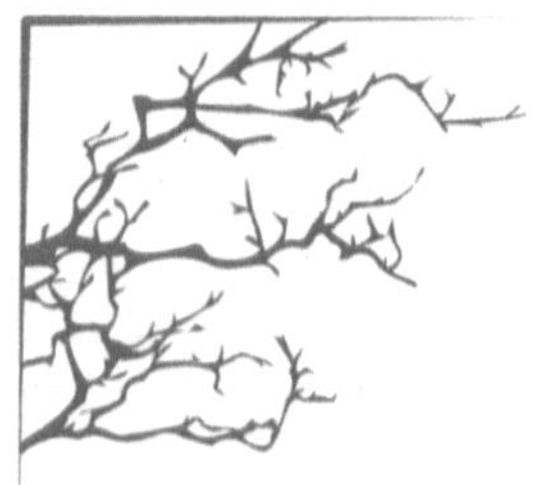

Chapter 10

Hannah

We've been running for two nights straight, only stopping to hide from the sun, when the sun wasn't out we were running. We ran through forests, rivers and plains. We climbed up mountains, valleys, and ravines. My clothes, were muddy, ripped and torn, and my skin was bruised and cut. Every muscle in my body ached as I kept up to Zane's feverish pace to put distance between us and his tribe in New York. When we finally stopped running, we were in a forest outside a small town in Utah.

Placing my hands on my knees I gasp for air.

"Zane, I can't go on much longer."

He nods taking deep breaths himself.

"I know. I think we've put a good amount of distance between us and the tribe. We can rest for the night before we must move again."

"Great. Any ideas on where to say. I'm not picky."

Zane smiles at me. "Follow me."

We run up a hill towards an open cave. Zane peeks his head inside the dark caverns. "This should be good."

"Good." I grin. I sit on a nearby rock and lean against the cave wall. "A perfect spot."

Zane nods. "You smell that?" He asks.

"Yeah, dinner."

Zane nods. "Come on. Let's eat."

We leave the cave an run about a mile away from it, to find lonely bar. It was full of patrons as country music blared from the speakers. Walking in everyone's eyes were glued us as we walking into the bar. The bartender walked up to us and asks, "what are you having?"

"A red wine would be nice." Zane replies.

The bartender laughs. "Now I know your from outta town. We only serve beer and whiskey here."

Zane laughs. "Two beers then." The bartender nods and hands us two bottles.

"Ten dollars."

"Keep the change." Zane replies, giving the bartender a twenty. He nods taking the cash and then walks over towards another patron.

"Thanks," I reply taking a sip.

"Welcome," he grins doing the same. We both turn to take in the atmosphere of the bar. Most people are line dancing and having a good time.

"Hannah…there's not many good options for us."

"What do you mean?"

"Typically we only go after criminals, but honestly it seems like good people here."

I bite my lip looking around.

"Damn you're right. Perhaps just this time, we go after an innocent?"

Zane raises his eyebrows. "An innocent? What happened to the vampire afraid to take a life?"

"That was different. Now it's about a survival. We can't fight what's coming for us if we're too weak. You risked your life for me. The best I can do is lax my mortals right now. Later, we will keep an eye out for criminals, but tonight we feast."

Zane nods.

"So who do you want?" He asks.

I search the patrons until I see a group of three men. Focusing on them I can hear their conversation. They are talking about which woman in the dance floor should they sleep with. Through their disgusting dialogue, I learn that one of them is planning to roofie one of the woman's drinks, giving me even more incentive to kill them. In between ease dropping, one of the men and catches my glance and smiles at me.

I turn back to Zane and whisper, "I think I got one. Those three guys over there."

"Yes, I hear them."

"They'd make a good meal, right?"

" I believe so."

"Stay here, Hannah. I'll enchant them."

"No, wait. They're guys."

"What is that's supposed to mean?"

"Like the drug dealer, guys only think with the thing between their legs. Don't worry, about me. I'll met you in the cave."

"Are you sure?" He asks. He leans forward and touches my hand.

"Yeah, I'm good. See you soon." I wink.

He grins and finishes his beer. Getting up he stares at me once more before leaving the bar. Once he's gone I take a deep breath and approach the three men. As I do, their smiles get larger.

"Hi..." I say in a flirty tone.

"Sup. That black guy with you?" One of them asks.

I shake my head. "He tried to be with me. I told him to beat it."

The man in the center smile grows larger.

"Not a enough man for, yah?"

I shook my head, batting my eyes at him. No, but I have a feeling y'all will be."

"Y'all?" The one on the right chuckles.

"Yeah. All three of you. I'm down to get freaky if you are."

The three men all share the same lustful look and the center one replies, "you wanna get out of here?"

"I'd thought you'd never ask. Follow me fellas."

Just like that, all three men are drooling over me. Never doubt a woman's curves. They are more powerful than any vampire magic.

I lead the men towards the cave near the bar. Along the way, they were a bit touchy feely, but I didn't mind. It is all a show. A few gropes and kisses are fine. It's all apart of the allure.

When we arrive at the cave, I can sense Zane towards the back of the cave. I knew he was waiting to pounce on the first guy.

Leaning on the cave wall, I smirk at the men. "Whose first?"

All three men laugh and from the distance I heard Zane say, "I'll take first bite."

Their laughter halted as Zane appeared from the shadows. His eyes were black and his fangs were out. The three men scream from the devilish appearance of Zane. They attempt to leave the cave, but I quickly jump in front of them. My fangs are out as I lick my lips at my next meal.

"Where are y'all going in such a hurry? I thought you all wanted to get freaky?"

Zane leaps in the air, tackling on man to the ground. His screams echoed in the cave as Zane drains his blood. Before the others could react, I am on top of the next man drinking his blood. The warm copper taste makes me groan. I didn't realize how hungry I am until his blood hits my tongue.

Looking up at the last man, he trembles with fear, cowering on a wall nearby. Standing, I wipe my face and grin at Zane.

"You first..."

"No, I insist. It's your catch."

I smirk and before the man can flinch I am on top of him. Zane joins in, drinking the man's blood. As we share a meal, we can't help but to smile at each other. It was twisted and dark, yet romantic. Feelings that I thought would never come are suddenly starting to emerge for Zane. Looking at his face covered with blood. I'm turned on. Dark eyes, gory fangs, blood stained ripped body. Every inch of him makes my body flutter. I'm not sure what's coming over me, but I do know, I want to fuck Zane.

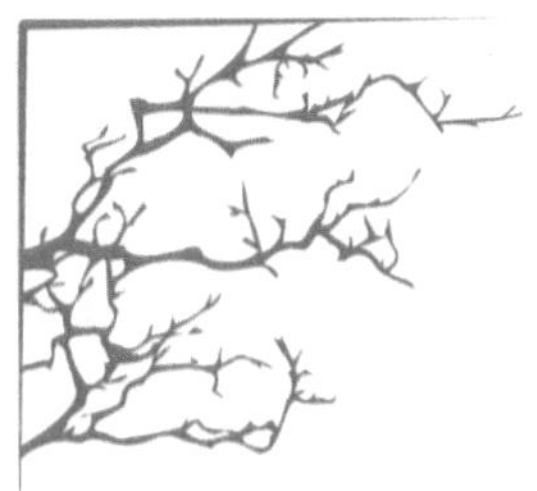

Chapter 11

Zane

After our meal, we buried the bodies near the cave. The graves were shallow, but we didn't care about anyone finding them. By the time they're investigated we would've been long gone.

Covered in dirt and blood, I walk towards a nearby stream. Not thinking, I strip naked and dive in the cool refreshing stream.

When I emerge from the water, I spot Hannah removing her clothes as well. Seeing her naked pale curves makes my stomach twist. My body aches watching her tip her toes into the current. My lust for her is overwhelming, and I was sure she could feel every emotion I was emitting.

Hannah dips her head below the water and swims towards me. When she re-emerges, she brushes her wet blonde hair back and smiles at me.

"Do you mind if you wash my back?" She asks, placing her blonde hair on her shoulder to reveal her smooth bare back to me.

"Sure." I reply. Swimming close to her, I scrub off the dirt and blood off her soft porcelain skin. As I did I couldn't deny the electric feeling that surge through my finger tips.

"You want me to wash you?" She asks.

"Yeah," I turn, allowing her access to my back. As her fingers slid down my muscles, I swear I hear her breathing deeply. Focusing, I can feel the strong connection grow between us. It is magnetic and undeniable. It takes all my power to keep from kissing her.

We separate and continue to swim around each other. Our gaze is unbroken, studying each other. We both want the same thing, but neither of us want to make the first move. I remind myself of the promise that I made to her.

While we are mates and bonded for eternity it was never my intention to be physical with her. I didn't want to put her in a situation to question that loyalty, yet, seeing her naked, feeling her touch, and smelling her feminine musk drove me insane. I try to fight the sensation that is coming over me, but it's a losing battle.

We are both silent until Hannah smirks, "that was a hell of a meal." Her smile makes my head spin. I could look at her smile for the rest of my life.

"Yeah, their blood was delicious. You did well drawing them over. The fact that you didn't have to enchant them is the most impressive thing. That's twice in a row you offered sex to men and they just followed."

She giggles. "Zane, like I said. Never underestimate the lure of the female body. It seems like I captured them and *you*."

"Me?" I scoff.

She laughs and nods. She swims closer to me. We are a mere inch apart. Her close proximity is making my body tingle. She grins as if she knew what her beauty was doing to me.

Of course she knew. It didn't take our physic emotional connection to know my desire for her. Even though I try to resist it, there was no denying that I wanted her.

"Yes, *you*. I saw the way you stared as I approached those men. I even detected a bit of jealousy from you. I detected it before too, when I lured that drug dealer away."

"I wasn't jealous."

"You weren't?"

"No, not at all."

"Well that's strange. Because before then, when I felt your feelings, I always knew what you felt. Fear, anxiety, happiness, lust. I've felt it all."

"Nope. Not true. I wasn't jealous."

Hannah closes the gap between us and places her arms around my neck. The feeling of her wet supple skin on top of mine is unbearable. She grinds her voluptuous hips across me and it's pull is undeniable.

"Just admit it. You were jealous." Her eyes bat at me in a flirtatious manner.

Fuck me...she has me under her spell now.

"I wasn't." I reply in the same tone.

"So, if I go back to the bar, and find another man, you're saying you won't care?"

"Not one bit."

"And if I kiss them?"

"Nope. I wouldn't care."

"Now, I know you're lying."

"I'm not. I made you a promise. Nothing physical."

"What happens if I want the physical?"

"Hannah, what are you saying?"

Hannah smiles at me and leans forward. Feeling her lips on mine I groan. For all the powers that I have, for that second I feel powerless. I am hers. At this moment, she can do anything she wants. That spark that we share is undeniable. That feeling that we have is intoxicating. It's addicting and raw. Her kiss leaves me breathless, wondering how I became so lucky.

"I want you." She whispers.

"Hannah..."

"Fuck me." She begs.

I growl and letting my basic instincts take over. I became hard and grasp her ass. Lifting her, I place her on top of me, and thrust deeply, entering her. We both groan from the sensation that is taking over both of us.

Connected, she wraps her arms around my neck, and nuzzles her head in the nape of my neck. At a feverish pace, I pump in and out of her, I can hear her moan my name. It is animalistic. It is raw. It is pleasurable. It is everything I want.

That feeling of burying myself in her folds is like no other. She is soft, she is wet, she is warm. That feeling of skin to skin contact. That feeling that I craved since I laid eyes on her was finally here. She is mine. She is all fucking mine.

We fill the air with the sounds of our love making. The sounds of splashing water and her moans make the birds crow. Her voice echoes in the woods. If someone is looking for us, they could have easily found us, but I didn't care at that moment. Let them come. She is finally mine, and I didn't give a damn about anyone hunting us.

Our lips are pressed together as I take her. I can still taste the blood of our latest victims. Her tongue swirling across mine only makes me want her more.

"Zane..." she whimpers.

Hearing her pleasure gives me strength. I double my pace taking her hard. The once still water becomes rough like the sea as our passion ignites in the current.

"Harder Zane. Harder..." Hannah begs. Her arms are wrapped around my neck as she bounces wildly.

I growl, my fingers sink into her wet white skin as I fuck her with fury.

"Hannah..." I groan.

Hannah moves her face from my neck to kiss me. Our tongues met and melt into each other. We both moan from the erotic thrill taking hold.

"Yes, Zane. Right there. Right there..." Hannah shrieked.

My hand adjusts it's grip, but I'm unable to hold on as she slips. She falls out of my hands, into the river, and laughs.

"Sorry about that..." I grin, picking her out of the water.

"It's okay. You good?"

"Yes. You?"

"Not even close. Come here."

She drags me out of the river and we walk to the muddy riverbed. She gets on all fours and spread her legs wide.

"Come on."

I grin. "I guess you like it dirty."

Hannah laughs, "I guess so."

I take her from behind. Our once clean bodies become covered in mud as we let our sexual desires take hold.

"Right there Zane. Right there." She mutters.

I bite my lip, and reach out to hold her neck. I lightly squeeze and she moans from my touch.

"Oh, Hannah."

"Zane...I'm nearly there."

I continue my quick bursts until she came. Right when she did, I feel her emotional outburst. With our connection, her orgasm feels powerful, taking my breath away. Seconds later I came too. Hannah moans feeling my own orgasm coursing through her.

"Wow..." Hannah gasps.

"That was amazing. I never knew the bonded mate's sexual experience would feel like that. It was like I was feeling your pleasure while I felt mine.

"Me too. Best sex I've ever had. Well worth the wait." She giggles.

"My thoughts exactly." I grin, leaning forward to kiss her.

Hannah laughs again.

"What's so funny?"

"We spent all this time trying to get clean, now we have to go back into the water to clean up."

"Ha, that is funny. It's well worth another dip though."

"I agree completely."

I help Hannah back up and follow her back into the river to wash our bodies once more. Once we are clean, Hannah looks back at me and asks, "Are you worried about the cops finding the bodies?"

I shake my head. "No, we will head north towards Canada and then cross the border. By the time the humans think about searching for them, we are long gone."

"Are vampires welcomed in Canada?"

"It depends on what tribe we run into. With us being so far away from our tribe in New York, I would think that any vampires we run into would turn the other way, but we are on the run. Surely my father and sister have spread word that we are fugitives and has a bounty on us. We must tread carefully."

"I'm ready to go whenever you are."

Hannah nods. "I'm ready."

"Good. We still have a few more hours till dawn. Let's put some distance between us and this town."

"Got it."

Hannah and I walked out of the river and got dressed into our tattered clothes. We were on the run again, but this time it felt different in the past. We shared something by that river bed. She became mine. We are finally one.

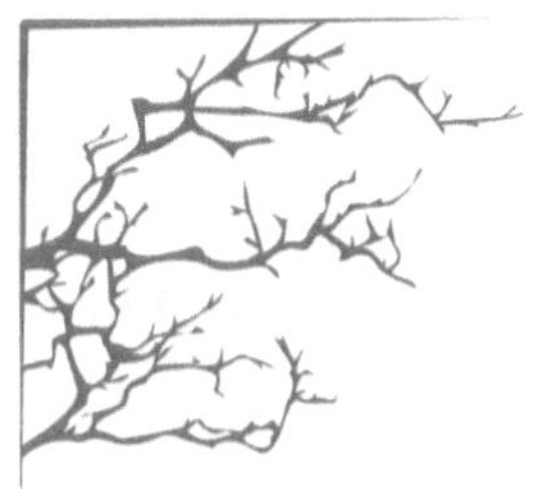

Chapter 12

Hannah

A day later we arrived in Canada. Right after crossing the border, we found an abandoned wooden hunting cabin. On the outside, it was rustic and small.

The windows are broken and the shutters are barely hanging on to its rusty metal hinges, but honestly after the last couple of days of sleeping in caves, this cabin looks like a four star hotel.

"We will stop here for the night."

I nod and smile at the idea of not having to sleep outside. I never was one for camping. Looking a Zane, we've both look like we've been through hell. After running throughout the night we were on going on fumes. We both need rest badly.

One positive is we've managed to find a change of clothes during our journey. After wearing the same dirty clothes for two days it was good to be in something fresh and not covered in blood. Zane is wearing a pair of dark jeans and a dark tank top. I changed from my leather pants and corset into a pair of dark jeans and blue tank top. We also got a pair of boots, which was helping with all of the cross country traveling we've been doing.

"We will leave a dusk tomorrow. We are just a few days run from Alaska."

"Why Alaska?"

"The tribe in Alaska has deemed it a peaceful area. Any combat against other vampires will face punishment. My fathers hunters won't be able to attack us, unless they plan on provoking the Alaskan tribes. I figure we find a cabin like this. Keep a low profile and ration our blood, we can settle down there."

A smile spreads across my face. "I'd like that. If I'm going to be a hermit, I'd rather be one with you."

A smile forms on Zane's face but soon morphs into a frown.

"They found us."

"Who?"

"Other vampires."

"What? How?"

"I'm not sure, but there's five of them. I hear them. They're running fast, coming from the south."

"Do we run?"

Zane stares at me. "We could. I for one am tired of running. We are close to an area where I think we can be free. I for one would like to fight for it, but if you don't..."

"No, let's fight."

"It's five to two. These aren't humans we can rip apart. They are vampires. They have the same strength and speed like we do."

"I like me chances. Besides I had a good teacher."

Zane smiles at me. He closes the gap between us and grabs my cheek. Feeling his fingers on my skin, I shiver.

"Whatever happens, if you see that we are losing the fight, you run. You don't worry about me."

"I will not leave you. We are in this together."

We both breath. Our bodies are both in sync. I place my hand on his broad chest and our eyes remain locked as Zane tilts his head down towards mine. Our lips intertwine once more as we share a fiery passionate kiss. Slowly, we break apart, but our eyes still linger on each other. Zane's finger strokes my chin. He didn't have to say a word to me. I know how he feels.

Our moment only lasts a few seconds before the other vampires arrive. Leaves and debris are kicked up as they halt in front of us.

Their hunting party consists of three men and two women. All are wearing black garments.

"Zane, your father has sent us. You and your mate have committed crimes against the clan. You are both under arrest, come now or else."

Zane balls his fists and spreads his stance. He controls his breathing and I can feel the adrenaline course through him. Knowing that he is going to attack, I prepare myself too.

"No..." Zane growls before leaping in the air, and tackling two of them to the ground. He manages to tear off one vampire's head off before being pulled off the bloodied corpse. He looks crazed covered in blood. He is growling and fighting two other vampires like he's lost his mind.

I didn't waste time, as I charge beside him, attacking the woman and man closest to me.

I punch the man hard, making him stumble back, and then dodge an attack from the woman. I quickly counter her attack with a swift kick to her gut. She doubles over and I counter kneeing her in the head. She crumbles onto the ground and before I could finish her off, the other man grabs me from behind and attempts to rip my head off.

I scream as a sharp pain goes through my body. Summoning my strength, I run backwards, pushing the guy into the tree. The tree shook from the hard impact and the man slumps down to the ground.

The woman recovers and charges at me again. She yells; sending a fury of attacks at me. Some land but I block most of them. Seeing an opening, I counter, striking her in the chest. She gasps and stumbles back.

I don't let up, not giving her a second to regroup. Keeping the pressure on, I strike her multiple times in the face, blood splatters from the powerful punches. She's disoriented and stumbles back and forth. I use the opportunity to finish her off by ripping off her head.

Blood splatters everywhere, bathing my face in her blood.

I wipe my eyes and turn to see the male vampire getting back up. He spits blood into the ground and gets into a fighting stance.

A small smile spreads on my face as I get into my own stance.

With a roar, he charges at me. I dodge his first punch and grab his arm. Shifting my hips, I rip his arm off and toss it to the side. He cries out in pain. He attempts to grab me with his other but I duck underneath his arm and grab him from behind. He wiggles and attempts to fight me off, but my grip is too strong.

Summoning all my strength, I yell and rip off his head, finishing him off for good. Blood springs from his body bathing me once more in gore.

Breathing heavily and dripping with my enemy's blood, I look up to survey the fight. Zane, like me, is covered in blood. Around him are three slain vampires.

We didn't say much. We didn't have too. I could sense every emotion emitting from him. At first it's relief, then it's lust. Strangely I feel the same. Standing there I ogle his blood drenched body. He stood like a gladiator among the dead vampires.

I couldn't resist the temptation. I had to have him at that moment.

I ran into his arms and he caught me, bringing my mouth towards his. I could taste the blood of the vampires we killed only turning me on more.

"Hannah..." he mutters.

"No... keep going." I beg.

He gives me a naughty grins and continues to kiss me. I moan as he licks off the blood on my neck. Breaking from his touch, I suck on his neck, slurping off the crimson beads of vampire blood on his skin.

Our lips rejoined in a dark and erotic kiss. We both moan captured by each other.

"Take me inside the cabin." I breathe.

Zane didn't hesitate, carrying me towards the building. He kicked open the door, and the wood splintered. Inside wasn't much, just a cot, a fireplace and a table. We didn't need much for what we wanted to do.

He takes of my tank top as I do his. Our bodies are twisted together as we circle around the cabin kissing. Nothing can be heard accept our moans. Our fingers feel like they are made up of pure electricity as we shed our clothes. His aggressive nature takes me as he pushes me against the wooden cabin wall. His large russet hands wraps around the waist band of my jeans, shoving my pants towards the ground. Feeling the cool air on my skin I gasp.

He tugs at his own pants and with one arm, lifts me up to his chest. Seconds later he's inside me, pinning me against the wall. My legs are twisted around him like a pretzel as he thrusts every inch he has into me. His groans are barbaric. His demeanor is wild. I am his, and he planned on letting me know that by the way he aggressively fucked me.

I groan as he feels amazing. He's so big. I love the way he stretches me out. No man could compare. My arms are wrapped around his neck as I bounce on his fully hard length. Feeling him pulse inside me I could hardly keep myself still.

We don't say a word as our eyes connect. Both of our mouths are ajar as our passions sweep us away.

We eventually end up in the cot. I'm on top, riding him. He's below smiling at me. His rough large hands are cupped around my ass, pumping me with every hard inch he has.

I close my eyes and squeal from the erotic sensations that charge through me. Opening my eyes, I rock my hips, taking control. Zane laid there watching my every move. His coy grin says it all, as he enjoys every second of my performance.

My hands explore every crevice of his body. They slide with ease as his dark bulky chest was covered in blood and sweat. My hands raise higher to his neck and he gives me a go ahead smile. I didn't need any further instructions as I choke him.

He groans, squeezing my ass tighter, fucking me harder. A loud clap of skin echoed in the cabin. The cot shifts and we break the bed falling to the ground. We don't let that stop us though. We were both so close.

We both came at the same time. As I came down from my high, Zane didn't stop thrusting until he's limp. When he was through, he smiles at me and pushes back a strand of my hair..

"Hannah, once again you manage to take my breath away." He breathes.

"Yes, it was wonderful, the fighting, the blood, the sex. I don't know what was better."

"Yeah, me either. In my hundreds of years, I've never experienced anything like that."

"Really, you never been choked out, while having sex, covered in blood from other vampires?"

"No..." Zane shakes his head.

"That's like a normal weekend for me."

Zane laughs. He shakes his head once more. He pauses and hesitates. He struggles with his next words as if they have the weight of the world.

He caresses my cheek making me shiver. "I love you." He admits.

"Zane..."

"You don't have to say it back. The fact that we're together is all I care about."

"Zane, I'm sorry. I really like you, but love..."

"I know." He cups my chin and kisses me. "No need to explain it. Come on. Let's get cleaned up and ready for the morning. At dusk we need to be on the road again. The sooner we get to Alaska, the safer we'd be."

I nod as I collect my clothes. Watching Zane do the same, I wonder if I'm making the right choice on not telling him my true feelings. I care, but to love is another step I don't know if I'm ready to take.

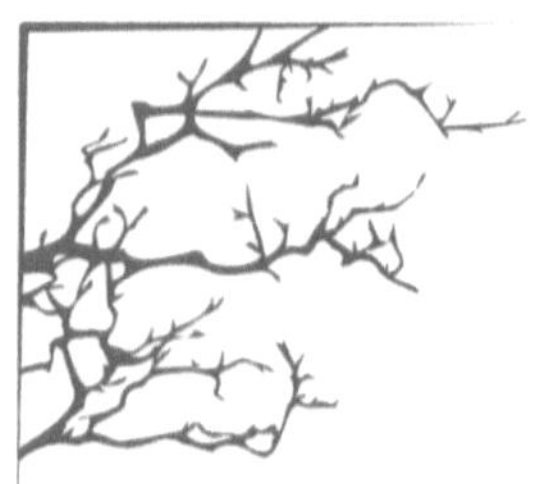

Chapter 13

Hannah

"Concentrate. Breathe. Let the transformation come to you." Zane whispers in my ear.

I take deep breaths with my eyes remaining closed. Zane and I are both sitting in the forest taking a break from our travels to Alaska. It had been a day since our fight in Canada. We were nearly a days run from our destination, and we decided to take a night off from the constant running.

Sitting in front of Zane, I could hear the wildlife of the forest and the splash of water from the the river. Slowly my chest moves as I focus on my transformation.

"Transforming into a bat is the hardest thing a vampire can do, but I have faith in you. It's all about the belief."

"Okay, I'm ready. I think I'm ready to to try again." I reply, standing up.

Zane nods. "Good. Try again."

I narrow my brow and focus on the horizon. I take deep breaths like Zane taught me and focus on transforming my mind, body and sprit to the animal. I take one final breath and then sprint forward. I take off at a high speed with the wind rushing though my hair. Every sense in my body seems on full alert.

"Now Hannah!" Zane calls out.

I leap in the air and growl as I summon my inner beast. I could feel my skin crawl and constrict. My arms and legs grow hair and I began to shrink.

I am doing it. I am flying. I am becoming a bat.

If it wasn't for Zane, I wouldn't have learned to do this. However, the more I think of Zane the more distracted I become. Instead of focusing on my bat, our last night in the cabin filters through my brain.

His admission of love and my lack of response replay in my brain. I feel horrible that I couldn't tell him that I loved him back. I mean I like him, isn't that enough? Why isn't that enough?

My thoughts of Zane spread like fire and just like that, I crash down to earth. My body skids across the forest floor kicking up leaves.

"Hannah!" Zane yells, running up to me.

He helps me up off the floor and brushes the leaves off me.

"Hannah, are you okay?"

"I am. What happened? I thought I was changing."

"You we're, until something stopped you. What was it?"

"I uhh."

Should I tell him how I really feel?

"I got distracted." I lie.

He nods. "Well try again. Remember, *focus*."

I nod and attempt to block out all thoughts of Zane. Before I could run, I feel Zane's hand on my shoulder.

"Wait..."

"What is it?"

"Vampires."

"More of them? I would have thought they learned from their lesson the last time."

"Not in the way you think. There's more of them. A lot more."

"Then we'd fight them."

Zane shakes his head. "This is a battle we will lose. I need you to run. Keep going to Alaska."

"Zane! No! I won't leave you." I cry.

Zane places his hands on my shoulders and stares into my eyes. "I do not want to be apart of this world knowing that your not apart of it. My father can do what he wants to me, but if he harms you, I will not be able to bare it. Please. Go."

"Zane!"

He didn't answer me back. Instead he gives me a passionate kiss. When we separate he cups my chin and smiles. "I promise, I'll be okay. Now we're wasting time. Go! Run as fast as you can. I'll try and hold them back."

I nod and run north. As I do, I can hear Zane and the other vampires fighting, but I don't dare turn back. Tears roll down my cheeks and I prayed hoping that Zane would be okay.

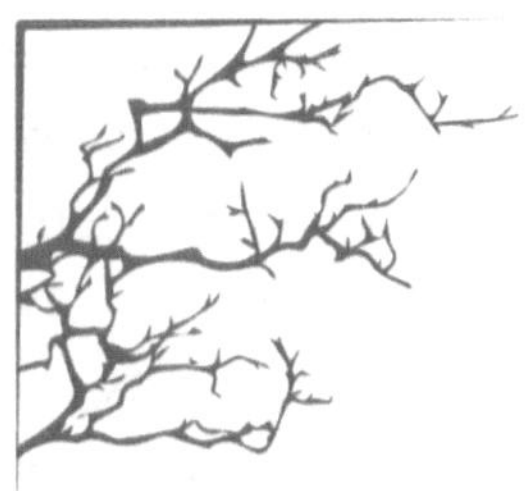

Chapter 14

Zane

When I come to my arms and legs are both cuffed to the wall. I growl as I attempt to break the bindings but the metal used was too strong. As I attempt to escape, my nose picks a familiar scent and I knew my father was on his way to see me. The door of the prison opens and my father smiles at me. As usual he is dressed in his formal robes.

"Son..."

"I am not your son."

"Really? Why the change of heart?"

"Attempting to killing my mate? You of all people should know. If mother was alive..."

My father slaps me hard and my head twists from the impact.

"Don't you dare speak of her..."

I spat blood and glare at my father. "She would be ashamed." I grimace.

My father hits me hard again.

He walks away, shaking his head.

"Oye told me everything. She told me how you saved that human and turned her. She told me how you went against the bylaws for your own selfish reasons. You talk about love as if you know it, you barely known this woman for a year, yet you claim to have fallen for her."

"I have. Three months with her feels like three hundred. I've have lived for hundreds of years, searching for a mate like her. Now that I've found it I will kill anyone in my way. You and Oye included. I don't want to be a kinslayer, but for her it's worth the damnation."

"You're a marauder without cause. We will find Hannah. I have my patrols looking for her. It's only a matter of time before they do. When they do, they will kill her and we will be done with this matter."

"You will not harm a hair on her. If you do, I'll kill you."

"Oh, son, you've made your threats known. Trust me, I do not plan on letting you out of this prison. This is where you will spend the rest of your days. Perhaps in five hundred years you will change your tune. Or I'll just wait another five hundred. I have all the time in the world, however your mate, Hannah, doesn't. She will face Oye and my cruel justice. She will die."

"Do it and you shall feel my wrath for all of eternity."

My father smiles at me before walking away.

"You hear me father!" I shout as the door is closed.

Alone again, I bow my head and attempt to break the bonds once more. It's no use as the metal is too strong, but I didn't care. I had to save Hannah. I didn't care how long it took, I will break these bonds and save her.

My mind is filled with all of these dark nightmarish scenarios of Hannah meeting her doom. I couldn't let my father or Oye kill her. The more I think of Hannah, the more I feel her. She is scared and tired. Those emotions give me strength as I keep pulling at the chains.

"Hannah...I will not let them hurt you. I will not let anything happen to you." I growl, attempting to break free. As I struggle I hear a familiar voice in my head.

"Zane?" The familiar voice calls out.

"Hannah?" I gasp.

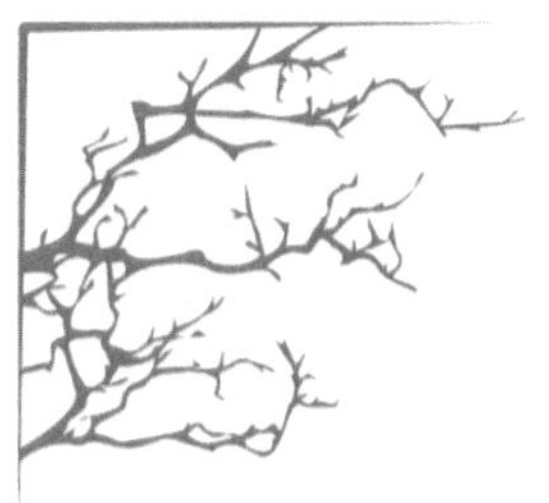

Chapter 15

Hannah

"Zane how is it possible that you can hear me?"

"It's our connection. They say when a bonded pair becomes strong not only can they feel each others emotions they can hear each others thoughts too. We must be doing that right now."

"Zane, are you okay? Where have they taken you?"

"I'm back in the manor in New York. My father has me prisoner. He's still out looking for you. Where are you?"

"I've made it to Alaska."

"Good."

"Zane, it's not good. I can't let you take the punishment for me. I'm going to break you free."

"Hannah you can't. The manor is a fortress. You can't break inside."

"Then I'll fight your sister."

"You can't. She'd kill you."

"She may. Or she may not, but I'm tired of running. If there's a chance that we can be together, I'm taking it. For once, let me save you."

"I don't need saving."

"Clearly you do. I love you Zane."

I breathe as I finally feel the rock that was weighing me down lifted. "Hannah..."

"No, listen...I was confused before, but now I'm am sure of it. I love you. You've always been there for me. I was blind, but now I see. You're the man for me. I choose you."

"Hannah...I love you too."

I smile at his admission.

"Hang tight. I'll be there soon."

"How are you going to get here?"

"By bat."

"Bat?"

"Yes. Before something was holding me back, but now there's nothing. I know what I must do. You need me. Hang on my love."

"Be safe."

I focus and begin to run. Feeling the transformation, I let the bat take over. My body shrinks and hair grows over my pale skin. I leap in the air and take flight. I am surprised at first, but I refocus, flying higher in the air. Determined, I realize my goal isn't just to fly, it is to save Zane, and I'd stop at nothing to save him.

I arrive at the manor and land in front of Oye who is waiting for me along with four other vampires.

Oye arms are crossed as she stares at me.

"It was a mistake coming here." She growls.

"I came here to challenge you."

"You mean you came here to die."

"If I die, I die. However, I will not give up the chance to be with Zane."

"Then you are a fool. Come." Oye commands.

The other four guards surround me and lead me into the manor. I follow them towards the fighting area in the home. When I stayed at the manor, Zane told me, this is where other vampires would challenge the tribe's champion. It's a large room, that has a second floor viewing area. Surrounding the walls are various African artifacts and a stairway leading to the second floor.

"Wait here." Oye told me and the other guards before walking away. Minutes later, Zane's father, Abdalla, Zane and Oye reappeared on the balcony above. Zane's father grinned at me as he stood next to Zane.

Zane eyes didn't leave mine as he stares at me. He looks beat and bruised. My fist clenches at the sight.

"What are to doing here?" Zane asks in my head.

"I'm saving you, remember?"

"It doesn't seem like it."

"Ha! I got this. I've learned from the best."

"And everything that I've learned, Oye taught me. She's the tribe's champion remember? She's the best fighter I've ever seen."

"Well, that's just great. A little heads up before would've been helpful."

"Hey, you've chose this."

"I love the vote of confidence, Zane. I love you."

Zane winked at me and replied, "I love you too."

My eyes focus on his father.

"I am here for your challenge. You said if I beat Oye, I'm allowed to stay a vampire. right?"

"Yes, do you accept?"

"I do."

His father's smile spreads and he nods. "Oye, you have a new challenger. Defend our tribe."

Oye stares at Zane before looking at her father. "As you wish father."

Oye jumps down into the arena.

She stares at me shaking her head. "Last chance, Hannah. Leave. Run. I'll give you a head start too."

I get into my fighters pose. "No, I'm tired of running. Are we going to talk or fight?"

A smile spread across, Oye's face. "A brave but foolish attempt. You have my respect, Hannah." Oye closes her eyes and takes a deep breath, before opening them again. With a mighty roar, she charges at me.

I square myself preparing for her charge, but I'm caught off guard when she transforms into her bat. She ducks under my arms and then transforms back into shape knocking me backwards.

I'm off balance, and it takes me a while to regroup. By the time I do, Oye is striking me again. A fury of punches keeps me from countering. Her strikes are powerful and takes my breath away. Within seconds I am already bleeding.

I yell, trying to grab her, but she's too quick. She ducks underneath my arm and grabs my head, placing it in a headlock. I try to break free but she's too strong. I can feel her pulling on my neck, preparing for the final blow.

This is it, I think. I look up at Zane hoping to take one final look at the man I love.

His eyes are narrowed. He shakes his head.

"Fight back!" He tells me in my head.

"She's too strong."

"Hannah, you've never given up. I have faith that you can. You're stronger than this. I know this. Now show them."

I nod and take a deep breath. I transform into my bat, slipping from Oye's grasp.

"What?" She gasps.

I fly high in the air and then dive towards her. I shift back into form and land a high kick into her jaw. She crumbles to the ground. It's my turn to attack and I didn't let up. I unleash a fury of punches and kicks.

I grin as I can see myself having the advantage. I draw blood making Oye stumble back.

She wipes her face and smirks.

"It's been a while since I've seen my own blood."

"There's a first for everything."

"Cocky. I like it." Oye charges at me once more and we trade blows. What advantage I had is gone as we evenly trade blows. Each hit we lay on each other is more powerful than the last.

I attempt to deliver a powerful haymaker, but Oye blocks it and delivers a solid punch in my gut taking my breath away. I double over and she grabs my head, kneeing me hard in jaw. I flip backwards to the ground.

Looking up Oye is hovering over me.

"It gives me no pleasure to do this. You've lasted this long, and it's clear you are meant to be a vampire, but I have my orders. I'm sorry."

Before I can react, Oye punches me hard in the face. She does this several times. I try to fight back, but I can't. She's too strong. My world turns black and the last thing I hear is Zane yelling, "No!"

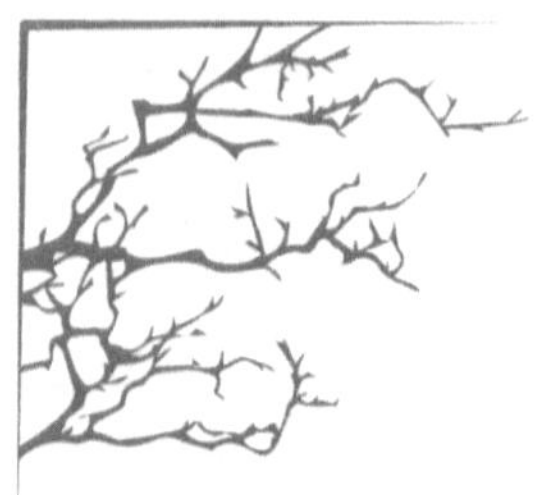

Chapter 16

Zane

"No!" I scream. I didn't hesitate, I didn't think, I just react, jumping down into the fighting pits. I get between Oye and Hannah and push Oye away from delivering her final blow.

"Brother! What are you doing?"

"I will not let you kill her."

"Move. Or you will suffer her same fate."

"Then I guess I will." I stand in a fighting stance waiting for my sister to attack.

Sister hesitates and then looks at my father. "This is madness! I can't fight my brother."

My father glares at my sister. "He has defied his father and the bylaws of this tribe. As champion, it's is your duty to follow the tribe chief. This is not for debate. Kill him now or be killed."

Oye glares at my father. "Then I guess we shall both die in this arena."

My father shakes his head. "It is sad that I must lose two children today, but by breaking the bylaws you are no children of mine anymore. You have both defied me and must die for your incompetence. Kill them all!" He yells.

Oye and I share a look before twenty vampires all jump into the arena. Oye and I stand back to back, with Hannah unconscious between us.

"So I'll take ten. You take ten?" Oye asks.

"Please, I'll leave you five." I joke.

"Cocky, brother. I like it."

The vampires all charge at us and we defend our position the best we can. There are to many of them as I block and defend myself, but I could tell that the battle isn't on our side. I manage to kill two and Oye has three dead bodies to her name as well.

One vampire manages to grab my arm and brings me to the ground. I attempt to escape, but another piles on top of me, dragging me down.

"Get off me!" I growl, tossing one aside, but another quickly takes the place of the man I tossed holding me down.

"Keep him there!" One yells as he circles around me. He grabs my head and attempts to behead me. I struggle but I could tell the end is near for me.

Just when I arrived to death's door,I hear a sweet voice in my head.

"Don't tell me you're giving up."

"Hannah!"

"I'm here, love."

Seconds later I hear the man behind me scream as he is killed. With renewed strength, I break from the grasp of the two vampires and kill one of them. Regaining my fighting stance, I see that Hannah has joined in the fight and is fighting side by side with Oye. They are taking on the remaining vampires.

Looking up, I see my father glare at me as he can see the tide of the battle turning.

"Father!" I yell. "We end this now!" I jump and land on the balcony above me.

"Fool..." my father mutters.

"Am I? I know I can end all of this with a single blow."

"You think those vampires will stop at your command?"

"I do. I kill you, I will be chief."

"You will kill you own father?"

"You didn't hesitate to kill me, your daughter or my mate. For that alone, you deserve to die."

My father smirks, getting into a fighting position. "Your confidence will get you killed."

"...And your arrogance will be your downfall." I prepare myself to strike and don't hesitate as I charge towards him. My father is quick, but I'm stronger. He lands several blows on me, but I didn't stop attacking . I am filled with rage. Nothing will stop me from being with Hannah.

I dodge his punch and kick combinations and land several punches to his gut. He doubles over gasping for air. I knee his head hard, making him twist to the ground. I stand over him, and glare at him.

"Last chance. Call it off."

"Never." My father growls.

He attempts to punch me, but I block his attack. I grab his arm and place him in a headlock and squeeze.

"I'm sorry father." I scream as I rip his head off.

I watch as his limp body falls, knowing that I had to kill him. It is the only way to stop Hannah from being killed. Grabbing his severed head I walk towards the balcony and toss his head in the center of the arena.

"As your new chief, I order you to stop this!" I yell.

The vampires stop fighting Oye and Hannah and look up to me.

"I've killed my father in combat and as written by the elders, I am your new chief. You will obey me or you will be killed."

The vampires all look at each other and then bow towards me.

"We are under your command, chief..." they all say in unison leaving Oye and Hannah standing. Oye smiles at me and then bows.

"Under your command." She repeats.

Hannah bows as well, but I walk up to her and pick her up.

"You are my mate. You bow to no one."

Holding her tight, I kiss her and then look at the rest of the vampires.

"Rise. Collect the dead, and leave us."

"Yes, chief." They reply.

Oye is the last one to leave. She places her hand on my shoulder and gives me a small smile. "Killing father was the right thing to do. He clearly wasn't in his right mind."

"Yes, it had to be done. Are you sure you will stay?"

"Yes, you need a champion after all. Other tribes will hear about this, some may want to take over our territory. You will need allies. You have my strength."

"Mine too," Hannah replies.

I smile at her and then my sister.

"Thank you."

Oye bows her head and then gathered my father's body. "I will prepare the funeral arrangements."

I nod and watch as Oye leaves the room. Looking back at Hannah, she holds me close.

"What now?" She whispers.

"Now, we live out our days as husband and wife."

"Husband?"

"Yes, will you marry me?"

I get on one knee and smile at her.

"Marriage is sudden isn't it?"

"Nothing about our relationship is conventional. Last I checked a year ago you didn't even know vampires existed."

"True. So what your saying is I can live happily ever after with the man I can love for all eternity?"

"Yes, be mine, Hannah. Be my queen."

"I do. I will be your queen and your wife." She grins.

I laugh with joy and swing her around. She giggles as she holds me close.

"I love you Hannah."

"I love you too, Zane."

With that final kiss, we lock our bond forever. With me as chief and Hannah by my side, no vampire challenged us as we ruled as partners and lovers for hundreds of years.

Don't miss out!

Visit the website below and you can sign up to receive emails whenever Remy Marie publishes a new book. There's no charge and no obligation.

https://books2read.com/r/B-A-HZLI-UIAPC

BOOKS 2 READ

Connecting independent readers to independent writers.

Did you love *Taken by a Vampire*? Then you should read *Short & Sweet Interracial Romance: Bundle # 1*[1] by Remy Marie!

Read five short stories all about interracial love!

This collection includes the following previously published titles:

Finding True Love

Wanting to find true love, Gina signs up for an online matchmaker. She gets matched with a black man, named Kyle. She is hesitant at first but soon finds out that true love comes in many shapes and colors.

My True Love

Rita once thought she knew. She thought she would be with that man forever, until he broke her heart, but life has a way of revealing it's true motives. In one night, Rita sufferers through heartbreak, but also learns who her true love really is. This is her story.

---

1. https://books2read.com/u/3RYnaD

2. https://books2read.com/u/3RYnaD

Always There

Growing up as a kid, I always thought I would meet my true love. I would have this magical romance where everything was perfect. However, life doesn't work like that. Instead of meeting my true love and living happily ever after, I have a kid with a deadbeat and get evicted from my apartment.

My life couldn't get any worse. Out of options, my best friend offers me a place to stay. Little did I know that my love life would turn upside down. This is the short story of how I found my true love.

The First Date

Sharron Carpenter is nervous as tonight is her first date with Brad Williams, a handsome single parent she met on a dating app. The two have already had several video calls, through their online dates, but tonight is the first date at a restaurant. Do sparks fly between the two, or does the date end on a sour note?

Runaway With Me

In the 1960s interracial relationships were still illegal in many southern states, despite this Malcolm and Jane fall for each other. However, outside forces will push this couple to their breaking points. Will this interracial couple's young love survive?

Read more at https://remymarieromance.blogspot.com/?m=1.

Also by Remy Marie

Short & Sweet Interracial Romance

Short & Sweet Interracial Romance: Bundle # 1

Finding True Love

My True Love

Always There

The First Date

Runaway With Me

Standalone

The Prince's Bride

What is Love? Part 2

Hot Summer Night Baseball

Taken by a Vampire

Watch for more at https://remymarieromance.blogspot.com/?m=1.

About the Author

Remy Marie is a romance author who loves to write about charming heroes and brave heroines. While writing never came naturally for Remy, he continued to strengthen his craft, by constantly reading and writing. If he is not writing or reading, he is usually watching TV with his supportive wife, aggressively cheering for his college and professional sports teams, playing video games, or crunching numbers at his daytime job.

Read more at https://remymarieromance.blogspot.com/?m=1.